Sæsq'ec:

A Controversial Account of a Bigfoot Attack

STEPHEN PATTERSON

DISCLAIMER

The following is an account of a Bigfoot attack as related by one survivor. Some names of people and places have been fictionalized to protect the privacy of those involved.

It is important, in the case of this contentious recounting of events, to make a special distinction for readers about the classification of fiction—which implies the author claims no responsibility to the truth.

By the end, you'll understand why.

Contents

FOR D

INTRODUCTION

The 1970's were particularly busy years for Bigfoot enthusiasts. Countless hoaxes and wrongly identified animals or animal tracks gave believers and or witnesses to the hairy anomaly international attention. Almost every continent has their own version of the cryptozoological beast. Some people think the spread of "Bigfoot Fever" can be attributed to the zoologists, anthropologists and any other reliable specialists who found the notion so preposterous they didn't even deem it worth their while to debate the issue, at least publicly.

Regardless of skepticism among most in the scientific community, a staggering number of people consider Bigfoot's existence probable or definite—something in the neighborhood of twenty-one to twenty-nine percent.

Why so many? Why do more people believe in ghosts and UFO's than global warming? I have a simple theory.

Once upon a time I would have said it's because there's little fancy, whimsy or wondrous mystery remaining in the world to give us something to dream about or fear. Much in the way modern people hold onto the possibility of extraterrestrials and ghosts, our ancestors had werewolves, zombies, vampires, witches, goblins, fairies, and countless other beasties to lend a little magic to the dismal monotony of our aspiration driven, orderly, ordinary, and reasonably safe lives.

You can be bothered by the dark, for no apparent reason, and the thrill is just plain fear—or, you can be afraid of the dark because you feel the presence of a diabolical entity that knows everything you're scared of.

i.e. It makes us happy.

While watching television the other night I happened upon one of these reality shows about trying to find or capture a Bigfoot. My wife and I exchanged looks and watched on as modern people carried on about a being most people write off as the most unbelievable of the improbable. Forty years earlier I'd shook my head the same way over articles in the paper offering rewards for evidence of such a creature. I wondered what started it up again.

Having started working for a Spokane daily as a delivery boy when I was eight in 1929, I have technically worked for newspapers for sixty-three years. I treasure the investigative process, love fact finding and drilling people for information and so could not resist looking into why this was happening again. What I found out will likely come as no surprise to anyone. The interest in Bigfoot, or whatever name people use for it, has *never* waned.

The truth is *I* stopped looking, like most people, when I didn't want to see anymore—not because I found no credibility to the stories and was sick of hearing about it, but because the choice to believe in *them* or not wasn't a luxury I had anymore.

Them? There are a lot of names for what they are: Abominable Snowman, Skunk Ape, Momo, Mey-Teh, Yeti, Raksha, Kikomba, Hairy Man, and countless others— most famously are Bigfoot or Sasquatch, a bastardized version of Sæsq'ec. That's a lot of names to call them without really telling us *what* they are. There are those who say aliens or demons, while others are convinced Sasquatch are Neanderthals, Meganthropus or Gigantopithexus. Some people even theorized that the famous Anglo-Saxon monster Grendel was actually one of these creatures.

Some people devote lots of time, money, and energy in pursuit of the Bigfoot legend. I can only assume these people are just more desperate for their existence than others. I can tell you this. Nothing about thinking if they exist or not makes me happy.

Why?

If you've read the title of the book you're reading I think there's very little room left for "why". Maybe it's time to get to the point.

Some of the things you're about to read implicate a number of people, including myself, of some wrongdoing. Some of those people are long dead and some don't have the sense left to even tell you who they are. Some of those people were bad, some of them good, and you might not know which one I am by the time you finish hearing what I've got to tell you.

To be fair, after all this, most days even I don't know which I think I am.

The point is that I worry people might get up in arms about what happened, but the fact is, this was a long time ago and I don't think anyone needs to go running off after any of the people involved—probably only if you were from there would you maybe be able to figure out who I'm going to talk about anyway. For these people's names and sakes I can only let you know what I think needs knowing and I'm only telling because I think it needs telling.

So before memory fails me, health fails me or courage fails me I'm going to record what really happened near the small town of Palmer, Washington 1983.

Sæsq'ec:

A Controversial Account of a Bigfoot Attack

CHAPTER ONE

In 1983 I was semi-retired, eight years earlier I moved up to Mariott, Washington from Spokane, after taking an early retirement from the Spokane Orator. My wife, Rose-Marie, and I had wanted to live closer to our only daughter and her family, who lived in Mariott, a small town of one-hundred-some people in Okanogan County where her husband worked for the D.O.T. and was away from home for long spells. Being able to see the grandkids daily and be a little company for our own kid seemed the right thing to do with our twilight years, but I wasn't ready for the easy chair and started working part-time at the nearest paper thirty minutes away, in Palmer, covering stories a hell of a lot different than I was used to in "the city".

There are a few things you need to know about Okanogan County. At about 5,300 square miles, it's the third largest county in the continental United States. The largest city, Omak boasts a population of about 4,500 today, but there were 10,000 fewer people in the county back in the eighties—the biggest city was smaller then.

One of only seven police departments disbanded about a decade ago and now, under contract of the Sheriff's Department, enjoys an as yet unheard of force of three deputies of the county's thirty-two.

In general, Okanogan County is considered a safe place to live, with a good start to the first decade in the twenty-first century with only three murders.

In 1983, for the whole county, there were about ten or twelve police officers and maybe twenty-five or fewer deputies. In Mariott, where I lived, and Palmer, where I worked, there were small offices in town, open eight to four o'clock, where a deputy or two and a secretary was stationed on behalf of the Sheriff's Department.

Larceny was and is the biggest crime problem in the county. So when five members of a family are slaughtered during a weeklong camping trip every officer or deputy in the area responds—in this case, that meant two deputies, two police officers and a sheriff.

At 5:44 on the morning of Wednesday, August 3rd of 1983, I was awakened by a call from my boss. Those days, remember, there weren't cordless phones everywhere—I believe the first cellular phone call was made only that year—and we'd only one phone to the house, so I was in a bastardly mood by the time I followed the shrill-drilling metallic rings to the kitchen. It could have been God on the other end of the line and I would have snapped at Him.

I barked, "What?!?," into the line.

I can still hear the tired gravel in the voice of my boss, who had been awoken even earlier than I.

"Some wacko went nuts and murdered a family camping at Buckhorn Park. The bodies are being bused to Connolly where they have the facilities to handle it."

"Jesus," I feel guilty to this day because I was thinking more about how my wife was still and unfairly asleep and cozy in bed than feeling anything about what my boss just told me. Murders didn't happen here. So you'd think I would have been alarmed, excited, interested, curious, horrified, but I wasn't. Maybe I'm jaded, but I just felt tired. "Any witnesses?"

"The killer."

People were starting to say "duh" more those days, after apparently losing some popularity after the forties, and I almost threw it at him, but then he added:

"It's the father."

I had covered more than one murder in my day and so the news lay pretty flat on the line.

Yeah, I thought. *It usually is someone they know. That's why the police check them first.*

"So he's singing?" I said.

"Get him to sing to you," my boss was saying next, but wouldn't be saying for long. It would still be days before all the notes to that particular song would be played out, but even before they had, all those involved were fiercely sorry to ever hear it.

Not surprisingly, in this thinly populated county, I was the first reporter to get wind of the event that would lead to one of the most controversial Bigfoot claims since the Gimlin-Patterson film. Though widely unpublicized and with scarce surviving documentation, it got a lot of attention in the small community where it all happened. Attention equally divided, at first, into figuring out the truth and then concealing it.

In the meantime, my first priority was to get an interview with the father.

It was a bit of a drive to the Connolly hospital. The first thing I noticed, once I arrived, was how stricken the nurses looked. Accidents and such—they had seen. Murder—never. Not here.

I followed the energy to a hall with scattered loiterers—I scanned them for other reporters—seeing none, I entered feeling like Dick Tracy. The guy with the questions and the initiative to get the job done and take no crap from nobody.

The feeling flickered when I passed the cleaning lady's cart and found the middle-aged woman and a young nurse mopping up the floor with discolored rags. I didn't miss the mop with its handle propped against a hanging picture. Clearly, too bloody to be useful.

I was impressed that the suspect was apparently hurt that bad—and wondered how sorry he was feeling for himself. It occurred to me the blood could have easily been unrelated, but it seemed unlikely.

Both women looked up at me, both their cheeks were shining with tears and their faces a little gray—that was when my confidence faltered.

I pushed them out of my mind and asked a woman with a clipboard what happened, but someone else answered first.

Call it morbid, but I was disappointed when some guy in the hall mentioned offhandedly that the survivor of the mass murder was saying a Sasquatch did it. Regretfully, the first thing out of my mouth to this stranger was, "So were there any deaths or not?"

"They already took away sis and the kids," said the weary looking man, whose eyes now flared up with anger he didn't seem to have the energy to accommodate.

"So your brother-in-law is saying they were all attacked by a *Sasquatch*?" I was still too belligerent for tact. Just two weeks earlier I received a letter at the paper asking for a reporter to look into a story. They enclosed a letter describing their brief encounter with the beast as well as a photograph as evidence (see ARCHIVE). My mind flew to conversations I had with a friend regarding what he described as hysteria when assigned to cover the sighting of a bigfoot-like creature in southern Arkansas about ten years earlier. For the whole of almost a decade before and after those series of events the world was captivated by "eyewitness accounts" of such a beast. I sucked at the air after the word fell out of my mouth, as if I'd cursed.

"He's sedated now," the man rubbed aggressively at his neck under somewhat long reddish brown hair—the word hippie came to mind—, "but that's what it sounds like to me, when he was carrying on."

"You don't think he's responsible?"

Now teary, bloodshot eyes flicked up at me with

more surprise than aggression. The blue-blue eyes were almost bioluminescently bright against the high color in his face and red in the whites of them.

He started answering me, but I left him without salutations when a Connelly Police Officer left the wing where I'd need access to soon if I was going to meet the father.

Introducing myself and what I was there for put him off to me; I expected it to. When he tried to brush me off I told him the truth, "People are going to want to know what happened."

"I'm one of those people," said the officer seriously.

"Can you give me anything?"

"How about some advice? This is a mess, why don't you give me your card and get on home. I'll give you a call if there's a press release, but we don't want this degenerating into a media circus."

"I'm the only reporter here," I pointed out. We both knew that would only be true for a short time if any of this got out—Sasquatch *or* family tragedy.

"Look," he put what seemed like a very big, very thick hand on my shoulder, "the rest of the family is on its way. The guy is out of it, now. There's a big mess up there in them woods and the investigation isn't even warmed up yet. I don't have nothing to tell you, see?"

"Meet me halfway—" I read his badge "—Duncan. Give me your first take on it."

"Most of a family is dead and in a mean way. That's all I know, friend."

The hand finally let go of my shoulder, though I'd feel the pressure of it for the rest of the day. What I had here was a small town that might deal with one mysterious death a year and it usually involved tourists or campers. These were wholesome people who didn't like dirt and gossip making their little hamlet look much different than the damn near perfect it almost was. Probably most small towns are like that.

Someone said to me once that there weren't enough people in Palmer for scandal. I remember answering, "There were only two people in the Garden of Eden."

Of course I knew, and most reasonable people would suspect, that the image of amity in the thinly populated "tri-city area" of Palmer, Mariott or Loup Lake was just a pretty dress it wore for strangers. Probably most small towns are like that. I was one of only three reporters at the paper, so I saw about a third of what would have gone in the "Legal" section if we had one.

When I heard that the man doped up in that bed, having recently been ranting about a man-sized ape with homicidal tendencies, was Doug Napier, I was barely surprised—which raised a strong conflict in me when very soon part of me found itself believing his account of the incident.

*   *   *

Back then hospitals didn't have the security they have now. I didn't have to get past keycards, security guards or even security cameras to reach the room where Napier was recovering, when I came back that evening. What I didn't know was if Officer Duncan Whatever was in there with him. I didn't suppose he would buy it if I told him I was just looking for the bathroom.

Tentatively I turned the patient room knob—another thing that's changed in hospitals I've just realized—remembering stories of people with arthritis not being able to get a hold of the smooth round knob and being stuck until maintenance arrived among other issues with the apparently un-user-friendly implements. I'm wondering now if I'm not too old to be doing this. Bringing up the past leads to a lot of digression. At that moment I was afraid that my path was leading me to a lot of trouble.

What it did lead me to was a semi-private room for patients with contagious diseases, probably the likes of TB or C-DIFF or something of the like. A cohort room, I suppose, but the other beds were empty.

To the last day I saw him, Napier denied waking when I entered the room, but I saw his eyebrows pinch ever so slightly. I saw his Adam's apple raise and fall as he swallowed down what I always thought was that deeper breath of waking. Then he breathed the shallow breath, of someone who wants to be perceived as sleeping, even though they should be breathing heavier. I would one day tell him that I appreciated that he didn't try to add a snore.

I closed the door quickly and quietly. The eyebrows pinched again. He swallowed again.

One fleeting glance through the small vertical band of glass was just about the sum of time I had between being just a reporter getting a story and a man looking for answers.

I'm ashamed that when I took that first real look at the guy that my initial thought was how I wished I had my camera. I shook my head as I made a mental note that at least one of his victims worked damn hard to stay alive.

An eye for an eye, almost, I also thought when I marked the savage scratches and broad discolored groves of bruises and lumps raised across his exposed torso, arms and head. What I couldn't see in those three realms were covered in bandages and a cast on his left arm. I felt a little satisfaction at the look of him and attributing the desperate work of a mother intent to save the lives of her children. Some people would take a look at this tall man with a rather powerful build and think of any woman having to fend him off and say, "Snowball's chance in hell." Then they'd obviously never seen what a parent is capable of when one of their children is threatened.

Good for her, I thought.

I took a folding chair from beside the empty second patient bed and when I turned back Doug Napier was looking at me. Not wide-eyed or even normal-eyed, but through the slits of tired eyes and or probably suspicious ones.

"Can't believe they don't have an officer watching you," I said. I know. Really funny.

The pinched eyebrows, a hard swallow again.

Guessing he hadn't been awake much or talked much more since he came in ranting, I almost tried my luck at telling Napier I was his public defender and I needed to start working on the case. Considering the ramifications of that, I decided against it, *almost* completely.

"Do you think we could talk about what happened up there? I know you're going to want to tell your side of the story before the police start telling their version of it."

The half-wrapped mummy answered with a blank

stare.

"What happened to your family?"

His dark eyes pulsed wider, eating a little of the overhead lighting and letting the teal-blue raise from the shadows for just a moment. A line formed between his eyebrows, his lips made a line too. His Adam's apple went up and disappeared somewhere behind his mandible a few still seconds before chaos.

A cry that was more like a roar erupted from his mouth that, at the time, seemed to open impossibly wide. Deep crimson flushed his throat and face as shining strips of tears tracked through the creases gathered on the outsides of his eyes. Veins rose on his forehead and his free right hand shook and clenched and opened beside it, undecidedly. It moved to still the cry, but couldn't. To hold his face. To rake his hair. To ring at the nothing over his chest where it probably expected a shirt or a blanket to be.

If the sound stopped or waned for him to draw a breath I missed it.

I tried to shush him, to calm him, because I didn't want to have to explain myself or the state he was in to the nurses who would come flying in at any minute. Luckily for me one thing hasn't changed in hospitals, then like now, I had plenty of time before I would have to worry about that.

Then I came up with the horrible magic words that would stop this show in its tracks:

"I know. I *know*. Look, I *understand*, you feel awful about what you did."

Like magic it did stop. Napier's back was twisted toward me and I could only see a quarter of his face. His hands, I noted to myself and to the pad in my lap, were not totally cleaned of blood. The right hand slowly fell away from its last attempts to still the involuntary scream. His forearm plopped into his lap and his fingers relaxed. It seemed like a long time before he fully turned back toward me, but when he did I had some concerns about my safety. It was hate. Hate and confusion and a second later maybe a little realization too, because when the hate and confusion were blinked away with the last of the standing water in his eyes, I think they became understanding.

It seemed like an even longer time before he finally said something.

He said, "No."

"Were you drunk, Doug?" Because, as I recalled, he almost always was.

I could tell he was trying to remember. I felt a smirk quiver on the corner of my mouth.

"*No.*"

"If not you, then who?"

He fired back, "How about telling me who the hell you are?"

I sat back, tapping the capped end of my pen to my lower lip. I knew I didn't have a lot of time to decide what to tell him—what I *knew* would get him to talk, or at least put the pressure on, or what would keep me out of the fire for the longest time. I did, however, know—or thought I knew—exactly who I was talking to.

The man laid up in that bed was a piece of shit. That's all I felt about him. Doug Napier was a hateful, no good, white trash bum who, for all I knew, spent very little time sober. He was the kind of man you'd cross to the other side of the street rather than cross paths with. To my recollection, at the time, he had more incidents of drunk driving than any other person in the county. With all the camping and shenanigans of people out to just have fun in the wild outdoors—that's really saying a lot, trust me.

I'm not going to lie about this either, I can be a little pompous and a bit of a bastard myself, I think. Maybe that would make it impossible for the interview to go anywhere, because we were both stubborn, ornery and believed what we believed.

I hadn't yet heard from the horse's mouth what *he* believed. I might get something completely different than he offered the police or his brother-in-law because he'd been laying there with time to think about what to say. To be fair, Bigfoot probably was the best thing he could think of, being hungover after a night of homicidal madness.

"Well I'm not with the census bureau," I chuckled.

He flashed me a look smoldering with hate.

Probably not the best thing to get him on my side, but I felt a little belligerent because I didn't care about his side of the story unless he was going to spill something good—I didn't really think he would. In the back of my mind I was telling myself that anything worth knowing I'd get from the police and the crime scene when I finally got out to it.

"Sorry, it's been a long day," I tried half-heartedly to wave it off, but it wasn't a fart—no one would look at someone that way for farting next to them. I don't think he was in any mood to hear a sad story from me about my early morning.

"I don't got anything to say," Napier sounded more

tired than angry.

I heard talking and footsteps approaching and jumped up so guiltily I don't think it was lost on him that I shouldn't be there.

"Darn. I just remembered I need to be somewhere. I will be seeing you around," I said with a wink that I *think* was supposed to be friendly.

His face and eyes dropped away from me. The pinching frown returned, his jaw set and by the time I reached the door he was holding his forehead like one bitch of a headache just came on strong.

A troop of nurses tromped past the window, startling me. Their soft soled nurses' shoes made them sound further away than they were. The door was closed and I was passing the next room before a nurse came along to check on Napier.

I didn't think it'd be fruitful to make the crime scene that night, even so, I waited in my car until I caught the weather. If we were looking at rain overnight I would have been up there to get what I could. With no precipitation expected for a few days I committed myself to rise early the next day too and check out the campsite where it all happened. I would have to come up with some blurb to print in tomorrow's paper.

On the way home I stopped outside the Sunoco station to use their pay phone. I dialed up the Mariott Sheriff's office and asked for Deputy Charlie Hoffman— the only person in law enforcement in the area, I always thought, that didn't perceive me as a know-it-all when it came to even the pettiest local crime, just because I was from the big city. I *was* somewhat of a know-it-all, I'd admit, but it was sometimes really frustrating to deal with people who didn't really know anything about "real crime". They didn't have the experience I had from my work in the "big city", which was one huge reason why I felt so good about my daughter living out here and why it seemed like the perfect place to retire.

Sometimes the monotony could bore me to tears or temper—the same monotony that drove some people to drinking.

It wasn't just teenagers complaining, "Nothing ever happens around here." In fact, most of the time when those words came out of local people's mouths it was grateful.

Back to the reason why I was calling up ol' Chuck, this was because he was a little enamored with the fact that I had lived in a large city at all, my experience with investigating crimes made me a Sherlock Holmes in his eyes, bless him. Not that I had a lot of cause to take advantage of the respect he had for me, but when I did he was more than happy to help since he understood the importance of my work.

What I understood about Chuck? He was one of few in law enforcement who would have been available or near enough to respond to this or any crime in the area. No doubt he was called to the scene right away, for two reasons. One, they'd need the help and two, because the Napier's lived in Mariott. Between the deputy in Palmer, which was closer and Ol'Chuck—who actually wasn't that old—who would have insight. He would have insight for me too.

As it so happened, there were only two deputies and two officers at the scene. Deputy Schaller of Palmer,

Deputy Chuck of Mariott and Officers Lane Duncan and Russell Kane of Connelly. Apparently the Deputy in Loup Lake was laid up with a broken leg at the time. No pun intended, but in hindsight, that was a very lucky break.

"Hey there, Deputy Hoffman—", I never called him "Chuck" to his face and I always humbled myself to his high social standing to let him feel I respected him just as much as he did me, "—I was hoping you could help me—"

"I expected a call from you," I was surprised to hear that he didn't sound all that excited since he almost passed out from the adrenaline rush when someone pulled a gun at an escalated bar fight. "Not going to be much of a story and I suppose that's the best thing."

"What do you mean?" I hoped I didn't sound as disappointed as I was feeling. When what he said fully processed, my disappointment went away when understanding moved in: I was going to get to sleep in tomorrow.

"Everything we saw at the camp and medical reports all come back that we had one mean son-of-a-bitchin' bear up there this morning. Brown bear probably, by what Doug said. He was just scared out of his wits is all and I can't say as I blame him. He was definitely too scared to lie—but scared enough that he might be confused."

"Brown bear?"

"Yeah and we're going to have to get someone out after it too. Park service said they've had a lot of complaints the past couple weeks about one being a little too brave and even more than once, probably the same one, being a bit aggressive too."

"How do they figure that it's the same one?"

"Whatever the campers said," Ol' Chucky sounded a little dismissive. What happened up there was a done deal as far as he was concerned.

"Have you questioned Napier?"

"We hope to get his statement tomorrow. Hospital said he wouldn't be in much of a state for business today."

"What did the coroner's report say?"

"Already told ya, said it was a bear."

"Right, right," I tapped my pen on the limp and abused pad of paper in my hand. The paper was rumpled with hastily scrawled notes, but only from the events recorded on pages before it. The indentations were ghosts of more interesting stories. The page I was looking at was blank except from the blue freckles my pen lent to the college ruled pocket notebook by tapping it.

To this day I don't know why I wasn't more enthusiastic. Bear attacks weren't and aren't common. However, there was a little voice in the back of my head saying I wasn't into *it* anymore. This was a sure sign that I was getting accustomed to the idea of being retired—that and the fact that I thought of sleep, recliners and what was on TV more than I had in all my life. To be fair, I didn't grow up with television. I was an adult before I ever sat down in front of the boob tube and was reluctant for a long time to get on that wagon, but here I was, on the dying embers of a multiple murder investigation, wondering what would happen next on *Knight Rider* and *Simon and Simon.*

Oh well, I figured, ready to haul my ass home to get some shut-eye—

"If you feel up to the drive to Connolly, I bet George Hill—" the coroner "—would explain all of it to you. I can call ahead so he expects you. I would rather people was scared of a bear that can be shot and gone so people can sleep than have people thinking Doug up and massacred his family on a camping trip."

Really? Drive all the way back to Connelly for a third time?

I sighed—in a shitty, long-drawn sort of self-pitying way that no one my age then should have done, "I suppose I ought to."

"Would you? I think that would help."

"Fine. Alright, goodnight. Keep me posted for when you're going to do the wrap-up interview with Napier. I'll let you know if I hear anything different, but you being deputy—I sort of doubt I will."

He chuckled in a boyish, prideful way and agreed with an, "Ayuh."

Before taking off I bought a gallon of gas, was about 1.10 at the time, and used the change—because I was out—to give a call to my wife. I secretly hoped she was sleeping. She wasn't and, as always, understood if I had to work late.

A lot of friends have told me how their wives nagged about being gone so much for work. My wife, Rose-Marie, never once bugged me about it, to my recollection. That being said, maybe I was more of a bastard than I realized, when I realized it. I always thought our marriage was admirable—my gut tells me what I always had was understanding not indifference. The idea then, that Doug Napier really might have brutally butchered his whole family, suddenly gave me the motivation to do this work with some fervor. I needed to hear what the coroner had to say. I needed to know that, while a piece of shit, Napier never did that. That no man could do that. I needed to know that one high-powered slug and a somewhat skilled shot would get rid of the real monster once and for all with no black mark of that scale on the face of human moral expectation. Yes. I needed to hear no father could do that to his family. I needed to know this was a safe place for my grandchildren and my own child to live. The kind of place my wife and I could live out the rest of our lives.

This was not my first time hitting up a coroner, pathologist or funeral director for information, but this was my first time doing it in Okanogan County…where this kind of thing doesn't happen.

By the time any of the top dogs in newsprint came sniffing for their chance to piss on the situation and make it their own, I needed to get some word out that downplayed the whole situation. I would be expected to churn something out by tomorrow's edition. Blame a bear like it could be nothing but. Blame a horrible oversight of leaving food out and I had enough whitewash until the next article. By then I would know everything the pros knew—the coroner, the police and, if I played my cards right, the horse's mouth.

CHAPTER TWO

I've already mentioned some differences between the way things are now and the way things were in 1983. One thing that has changed in some places is how much schooling a body has to have to qualify to be a coroner. Considering that these folks, in most cases, have the power to override a forensic pathologist, it's always struck me as funny—no, it's not funny at all—that more wasn't and sometimes isn't required for qualification. Sometimes you had to do the job if you were the lead in the law, the judge or sheriff for example. Every state is different. A lot of places these folks were just elected or were running the funeral homes anyway and were appointed the role. That was the case with the fella I was out to meet the evening of that early day in August.

I hadn't had a lot of reason to know this guy, George Hill, except that there aren't a lot of people in the area, so you get to know the "important" ones. The last time I talked to him I was covering for the guy who usually wrote up the obits and I needed some facts verified. Big deal, but I was hoping that Hill remembered me well enough that I could get somewhere toward the facts. It's who you know, right?

The funeral parlor looked like a house, largely because it *was* a house and still, in part, functioned like a home, as a lot of them did back then. I saw a figure at the large rectangular sectional windows on either side of the dark brown door. Against the gray house the door looked like the entrance to some everlasting, starless void. When the porch-light was flipped on to accommodate me as I approached, the light grabbed the slightly raised and sunken rectangular sections and lit the antique knocker that, after having just seen it as some ethereal rift, seemed to declare my overactive imagination with the hint of a snicker.

The sheer burgundy curtains sashayed like a cocktail dress as the silhouette, that reminded me of a sandwich with an olive on top, left the window.

The man who answered was a little younger than me and wore the weight of a worrier, which I hoped meant that he took his responsibilities seriously—I would later find out that he took them really personally too.

His dull brown hair was the most unfortunate color. It had no richness, no shine, a look of being matted while obviously being combed and clean. A shorter guy, his heavy sweater and gray-green corduroy slacks did nothing to help him look taller or leaner. It was about 80 degrees out and it wasn't exactly cool inside. For the moment I was perplexed at how he could stand it, but a little later that night he would point out that it's wise to dress a little warmer when you spend much time in a basement—and he did.

"Hi George, I'm Stephen Patterson. Did Deputy Hoffman get a call in before I arrived?"

"Yeah, yeah," he'd said, ushering me in with some urgency. Not the kind that says impatience, or busy-ness, or even the excitement of "I can't wait to tell you what I found out", but to keep the mosquitos out.

"So we have a mean ol'bear out in the park, have we?"

"Looks like it. I took a lot of pictures up there, comparing the injuries to photos of known bear attack photographs. I took some pictures of the campsite too and some partial paw prints the police pointed out, in case anyone asks."

"Sounds solid," I praised as he led me down an elegant, but home-like runner that matched all the other décor of the funeral parlor. "So why were they fingering Napier for the deed right away?"

"A few abnormalities," Hill said with a shrug, "but they're easy enough to explain too."

"Such as?" my curiosity didn't exactly peak, but I did want to know.

"There was tissue under June Napier's nails that wouldn't have come from defending herself from a bear, but very well could have come from defending herself from her husband—from what I've heard, I'd say that's so."

We entered the work room downstairs and the smell that accompanies sterile spaces responsible for anything rotting.

"It would be unethical to show you the bodies—" I almost rolled my eyes as he informed me. *When has that mattered?* "—but I can show you some of the photographs."

He started flipping through about half an inch of page sized photos while I looked over the table. There were notes, a few Polaroids, and empty foam coffee cups. There were also five pages with crudely drawn human bodies marked with notes regarding the injuries each incurred.

I lost myself for a moment, eyes glazing over the densely covered generic image of a male body, fixing on the notes in the corner:

James Napier – aged 3 – primary mechanism of death: repeated blunt force trauma to the head, likely the cantaloupe-sized rock found beside the body (see image 33)

"What's this?" I asked, lifting a sandwich bag up and out at shoulder level.

Hill looked up over the tops of the photographs, eyebrows barely raising in an "oh" expression as they fixed on the swatch of dark, reddish-brown hair resting innocently against the seam at the bottom of the bag.

"That's the hair we took from between Mrs. Napier's fingers. Had a literal death grip on it. Wherever she is, I hope it does her some good to know no one could have fought any harder than she did."

"I agree," I said, but no sound came out. I tried not to see the drawing of June Napier's injuries as I returned the bag to the heavily littered table. I was thinking that it reminded me of her brother's hair.

Time wasn't taken to collect evidence off the bodies or off Napier. Had that happened there would surely be more than the swatch of hair I was staring at through the clear plastic bag. Later conversations with Chuck would confirm it.

"So, see here?" Hill turned a photo toward me that clearly showed finger-like bands of bruises on June's forearm. Then one showing the black impression of a thumb on one side of her neck and the matching impressions of the fingers where they almost met.

"Jesus," I muttered. "So you think Napier beat the shit out of her earlier that night and then the bear came?"

"We think that might have been *why* the bear attacked. The loud noise might have provoked it if it was brazenly approaching campers, it may have already been in the camp and perceived it as a threat or it might have smelled blood."

I shrugged. I wouldn't know and it was some time before I'd ask someone who would.

I reached out for the rest of the photographs, hoping if I acted like I should have them then he would think I should too. Next, the stack of pictures was in my hand.

I assumed then, and have since, that I was so horrified by the images I saw because of the amity I projected on the area we lived in. It was an offense to my reality. In Spokane, if anything like this had happened in our neighborhood I think I would have experienced the same horror as I did looking at what happened to the Napier's. I saw a lot of horrible things in my life, but it was never personal, it was always "somewhere else".

"You think he hurt the kids too?" I saw similar

prints on the children and George Hill nodded. "So the bear attacks the sounds that scare it. Rips apart their tent. Savages the kids—the whole family—" I hold up the picture of the rock "—and this?"

"It's possible Doug was putting James out of his misery," the coroner replied, regretfully shaking his head.

"I see," I answered, leaning in to study a frame of the destroyed canvas tent and what appeared to be an elongated bear track beside a mangled aluminum rod. Or maybe a distorted human footprint. It was impossible to tell for sure, but I was thinking of a culprit, and not a bear, when I finally left George Hill's in the wee hours of the next day—it wasn't Doug Napier either.

Back in my tan '79 Ford wagon, I'm stuffing my hand into my jean pocket and hoping Hill won't miss the bag of hair.

CHAPTER THREE

It wasn't any secret to the people of our area that Doug Napier was a drunk. I was beginning to wonder what his brother-in-law thought of this troublemaker getting involved with his sister—or what anyone else in the family thought, for that matter.

I had a better look at the hair when I got back home earlier the morning of the August 4th. I'm no biologist, and would have a poor time pretending to be, but it was definitely hair, not fur, unless I had no idea what loose bear fur would look like—and I didn't really, but the texture was so much like human hair and if what he had in that bag was the fistful she took, I imagined if she'd yanked on a mess of fur, like she must have, it would have stripped a bigger mess than that. But if you tore at some fellas beard or head I'd think you'd get less from thinner hair. Maybe I'm wrong and always have been wrong about all that, but I was pretty sure I was going to be right about one thing—that I was going to find a mess of bare not bear footprints up there that would not match Doug Napier's feet. I bet that I would find that those blown-up photos of bear tracks in the brush to be the prints of a man walking tiptoe. I'd take my own pictures, thank you very much.

It might have been easier to blame the whole mess on a pest animal that got mean, but if somebody was responsible I wasn't about to see them walk.

I was contemplating these things and what I'd seen at George Hill's as I made the hour and then some drive out to the park.

My missus was giving me a hard time about not getting much sleep and being on a big story—though she was teasing, the fact that both were true had put me in a sour mood. The "on a big story" was something she'd only started teasing me about since I retired as there had been no such thing as a "big story" since. I'd always enjoyed it.

After my involvement with this incident was said and done, she never teased me about it again.

Maybe the problem was that I *had* covered homicides before. Maybe the problem was that in those cases I always expected, and or hoped for, a complicated mess of a whodunit story...so maybe I was looking for things that just weren't. Like I said, I'm no biologist or scientist or anything. Maybe sometimes things really are just that simple. Little did I know, this wouldn't be one of those times.

Rose-Marie had the good sense to stop me from walking out of the house with oxfords on. While I'd been cursing her out some for her teasing I was God-blessing her before I'd even gotten out of the car in the park's lot.

It was a cool morning, such as it is in August, ready

to be hot and humid as hell in a few short hours. A fine white mist diffused the morning sky while a denser fog lay in the pockets of lower ground like snow in the spring, when almost all else has thawed.

Approaching the park visitor center, I couldn't stop staring at signs indicating the way to the campgrounds. There were some really open, almost communal camping areas near here where kids could do activities with the rangers and have access to the few available amenities— like running water, little brick bathroom facilities and the gift shop that, like most, sold a lot of crap and souvenirs. I think the old-fashioned candy was the biggest draw for children.

The Napier's hiked to one of the inner sites. I wouldn't be surprised if this wasn't to avoid the stares demanded by Doug's reputation. I didn't want to start asking teachers, friends and neighbors what the couple was like, if the kids seemed troubled and if his friends thought he could do such a thing. You plant the question in someone's mind and they have to ask it to themselves. If they never would have questioned it before, you've made them feel like they should and that will never go away.

I was pretty sure that it wouldn't be long before I started to ask *somebody* something—that's about half of my job. I didn't mind being an asshole sometimes, if I was pushed that far or just felt like being one, but it was never my intention to leave a trail of destruction behind me. I have always been conscientious of the media's power to distort reality.

When I was just a little shithead, doing deliveries yet, I'd asked a reporter why everyone was saying this or that about this "no good" swarthy Italian guy. He turned to me with a wink and answered, "Because I said so."

I introduced myself to the ranger, Grover Meldrum, at the registration desk and told him why I was there, partially to avoid any hassles when I got to the camp and also to try and get around any parking fee or a day pass, which I did.

"Is it always this quiet?" I asked, gesturing to the nearly empty parking lot behind me.

"Regularly it would fill up just before lunch. People who come to picnic and swim. Most the rest of the visitors park at their campsites or at the parking lot halfway around the loop where the Napier's parked. It's closer to the trails where hikers go for camping."

"So that's not the path they took?" I point at the sign I'd been fixated on.

"Naw, that's just to Camp Area B. One of the more family friendly campgrounds."

I asked the ranger if he knew the names of any of the witnesses from yesterday morning, if any of them were still around. I wasn't surprised when he told me most of them left as soon as the police let them, but hopefully the police had taken more than just statements. If I could I'd probably want to talk to them myself—numbers and addresses would help.

"Can I get the contact information for the rangers who were there?"

"I can check," Meldrum offered with sudden somberness. It was different, it was about his "home" then. Someone in his "family" had been hurt by what happened and I knew that he personally knew who'd been up there to witness the aftermath.

"Is there anything you'd like to tell me about all this before I get up there?" I wanted to know.

"You don't want to wait for a ranger to take you?"

"Do I?"

"Well," his tone suggesting that he thought I was a lunatic or half-wit, "That bear's still out there, you know, and we asked everyone out of those camps until she's killed. If something happened wouldn't anyone be there to help you."

I considered this, didn't really want a ranger hovering over me, but, "What can I say? I hate to bother someone."

"Will be more a bother if we have to take a bunch of people from their work to find all the parts of you, right?"

"No arguing with that."

Then Meldrum got on the radio and went back and forth with somebody or bodies until he said so-and-so would be there in about ten minutes. I missed the name thinking about the gruesome image he'd just put in my head.

"I'm going over there to to make sure I have everything I need," I excused myself. "Thanks for all the help Grover."

"You bet, Mr. Patterson. I hope you can find some peaceful way to write what happened up there—to explain to people what an ugly fluke it was so people won't be afraid to be up here. There's rumors is all now and just upped the general warning on bears since all the campers are close by now."

"Well, we'll all feel better when that bear's put out of our and probably its misery. There must be something wrong with it."

"That's the way we figure," the young ranger agreed.

It was closer to fifteen minutes when a man, probably in his forties, with a face younger than the gray in his dark brown hair, showed up to escort me to the site of the attack. He was shouldering a rife and looked tense. I was correct in assuming this meant that he knew more than just rumors. I mentioned the Christopher George movie *Grizzly*.

"No. It's nothing so dramatic. What we have is a case of a bear that is probably sick. It's not thinking right, getting close to tents and campers. It'd been threatening, but not violent until now. We already had people out looking for it because of all the complaints."

"How do you know it's the same bear?" I asked as I piled into the park ranger's pickup which we'd take to the second parking area.

"It's skinny and mangy. That's going to stand out anyway, but it's odd in months when bears are working toward winter weight, unless they're ill. Sarcoptic mange does hellible things left untreated and dogs can give it to just about anything."

"You know your stuff then?" in my mouth tasted more like, "Can I quote you on that? Would I want to?"

"I manage most of the public relations between our guests and our residents. I went to be a veterinarian, but my grades weren't up to it. I like this work better than I think I would have that."

I asked about where he was from and a little about what was stumping him in school. He was probably the closest thing to an expert that I was going to have so I was grateful to have him along and said so.

The sun was obviously up a bit more by the time we parked by the hiking access to what this ranger, Paul Ketchum, called Camp Area H-3. The angle of the rays pressed the trees' shadows into a darker realm of shadow and made the penetrating light even brighter where it splashed and streaked across the forest floor. We were heading to lot 9 in H-3, where the Napier's were alive about thirty hours ago. It didn't look particularly inviting, to be honest I was never very outdoorsy, but it made me wonder how these guides and rangers could stand to do their work, especially when so much of it was by themselves, in a place like this…after something like this.

The remote parking lot had a Visitor's Guide stand stuffed with maps and brochures and one of those two-sided restrooms that just get vandalized the hell out of nowadays, if they're even still in service. Outside the restrooms was a water fountain that, thinking back, reminds me of the smokeless ashtrays in *Gremlins.*

"So what kind of complaints were you getting?" I ventured as we crossed the narrow park road and passed two small signs married to a sturdy metal post, one with a simple drawing of a hiker, the other with a tent.

"Mostly about it coming into their camps, or being in their camps. It matches up with what happened up here. A fella in one of the nearest camps said it was just about dawn when the screaming started. Most of the sightings took place at sunrise and sunset. Three different hikers reported this animal acting menacing on the trail, forcing them to turn back. One said it must have noticed her before she saw it and when their eyes met it dropped back to all fours and started smacking the ground with its front paws and grunting at her. Another guy said it took its aggression out on a tree, like it was having a temper tantrum—howling and shoving on it and dropping on its fours to give the ground a beating. Did a mock charge that turned the hiker back to the visitor's center. Still another person, a lady with a whole mess of kids, said she saw it standing upright and challenging just outside the clearing of their camping lot. She struck me as a little eccentric and needy for a little attention. You'll never believe what she claimed."

"What?" I tried to sound extra interested to encourage the thread to keep running while I took notes as fast as possible.

"She said it was clearly aroused and seemed engrossed with her. Said she figured it must have been standing right there when she'd went and relieved herself moments before just about where it was standing—that it must have followed her, liking her smell."

"You're kidding," I exclaimed, but wasn't really surprised. Conventional people are always the scarce ones.

"Then, of course, because this poor ranger was listening and rightfully shocked by what he was hearing, the lady started rolling that snowball until she couldn't push it anymore."

"Somebody's getting her husband a monkey suit for their anniversary," I waged.

Ketchum laughed in a grateful way that said, "Boy I needed that. Been a shitty week."

On the high note, we didn't talk much more for a long while, I suppose since we were going to be talking about a lot of bad stuff soon enough. He remarked on some things going on with the daylight or growth of things he thought was pretty. He pointed out a fox so far on the side of a hill I barely saw it.

It felt like too soon, for some reason, when we got close enough to the camps that he started telling me so and what to expect—that there was likely to be a lot of blood still. That the place was in shambles. That he didn't think anyone else had been up there since the police, emergency and the park services cleared out the remaining campers.

"You're not going to like what you're going to see," he warned as we passed the sign indicating what lots went left, right and straight ahead, like once we'd passed by he wouldn't get a chance to say so.

It was at about this time when I caught a whiff of something funny in the air, nothing I'd ever smelled before, but maybe a combination of several smells I'd never experienced at once.

"You caught that? Smells like pigsty, skunk and rot, don't it?"

"It sure smells like something…something bad," to be honest it struck a primal fear in me—like the instinct to be afraid of the dark or strangers.

He must have read my face, because he asked if I was going to be okay.

I didn't want to seem ungrateful for his consideration of how I might feel about this, so with a little nervousness, I don't know if I forced or not, I said, "This is my first animal attack story."

"May it be your last."

I had an urge to say, "Amen."

The little brown posts with white numbers marked the small empty lots. I glanced down at my notepad and then watched the numbers counting up.

5, 6, 7...

I could still smell the campfires. The grass was still matted from tents and sleeping bags.

8.

An overlooked metal tent stake caught the light among the dewy grass. These people were about twenty-five yards from the Napier's lot. They would have heard it all. Did they see the aftermath? Did they think about helping? Did they lay in their sleeping bags holding each other in terror, wondering why their neighbors were screaming and if they would be too?

I took a picture of the brown post at Lot 9. When I lowered my camera I took a moment to absorb what I was seeing and Paul Ketchum gave me a lot of room to do it. He'd actually taken the rifle off his shoulder and his eyes were noticeably busy.

"Did you see something?" I worried.

Ketchum shook his head and kept looking, "We know it was out here and there's still a lot of blood on the ground. It might come back, if it decides it missed a meal."

"It didn't eat on them?" I was surprised.

In a casual kind of way, the ranger replied, "Bit them a little."

I took pictures of the path before stepping into the lot. A lot of people had walked around in here, I was disgusted to see. A *lot*. Tromping around like a bunch of cows.

My eyes fell on the destroyed tent, noting the browning red streaks and spatters all over it, then I started to see that it was everywhere.

I took a picture of what was left of the print by the tent, which meant less than nothing now. What I saw might have been part of a big toe impression under the deep treaded track of boots. If the family was sleeping, there would be a lot of reason for bare footprints during and after the attack—even the night before.

There was a tremendous amount of blood inside the remains of the canvas tent. A black sticky pool, squirming with ants, lay in almost the center. There was a lot of blood near the back wall too.

The incessant hum of flies was felt in my flesh and made it crawl. It even made my brain feel crawly. There were simply thousands and thousands of flies.

"That's where Doug and Randy were found," Ketchum told me.

"Randy," I repeated—one of the kids. "What about the others."

"The only daughter, six, was discovered on the far left of the camp where it must have been dragging her off at one point. You could see where she slid across the ground there."

I could make out some signs of what he was saying and was taking pictures as fast as I could.

"Over there is where the youngest, age three, was found," Ketchum pointed to the woods between this lot and number 10. "It looked like he was trying to run away. Maybe get to one of the other camps."

"We found a flashlight and some blood in the woods at the far right side of the camp. The bear clearly took off that way, the flashlight might have been thrown at it and [the bear] might have had a lot of blood on it."

I nodded.

"Over there, by the fire, their oldest, Dennis. He was still alive at the time help arrived. Too bad he couldn't have held on just a bit longer because the doctors said the injuries didn't have to be fatal. He just bled too long, too much."

Through the lens I fixed on a large patch of grass packed and smudged with blood. It was about the size of my kitchen table. Even where people walked, the furrows dug into the dirt where it met the grass was obvious.

"Mrs. Napier," I said, not asked.

Ketchum nodded and finally came into the camp.

"We think she fought it for a long time. All of this is from it pushing her side to side as it was mauling her."

"And those?" I pointed to the gouges in the earth.

Paul Ketchum's intelligent brown eyes looked and then raised up to mine, "Her kicking feet."

"Was her brother up here with them?" I asked as I used up frames.

"No."

I took half a dozen more shots before he asked me why.

"I was at the clinic yesterday morning. He was already there."

"Oh," the ranger thought about it. "The family would have been called. He probably went where he was told they would go. If he lives over there, he would have beat almost anyone."

This was true.

I was thinking about Doug Napier's frown when a moment arrived to do a deep one of my own.

I was standing at the end of the camp, where the light disturbance of one heavy thing passing left the brush gently parted and the impression of a footprint on the ground. One would think there'd be little reason to smile where almost a fourth as many lives had been taken as hurricane Alicia would in a little more than a week, but I was smiling. Smiling like a jackass and burning up the last shots on one of my last rolls.

"What do you make of this, Paul?" I suddenly thought it was fine to call him by his first name.

His lean body slipped into the meager remains of space in the barely notable path. He crouched to get a better look, then stood straight and put his hands on his sides—the posture itself declaring he'd no idea whatsoever.

"Might be someone gimp, a foot disfigurement."

"That's a big foot, disfigured or not," I remarked. "Could the bear have been hurt and slid its feet funny."

The ranger considered this with a shrug.

"A bear would have done more damage than this going through the brush."

It was my turn to shrug.

"Huh," Paul grunted and scratched the back of his military style short hair. "I bet these are the same weird tracks Gus Omak saw on the trail by the north shore access. I guess I'm gonna have to stop giving him shit."

"Why'd you give him shit?" I laughed forcefully.

"He's always seeing stuff and gets other people

thinking they see stuff too. Wish he'd join us sometime and tell campfire stories, because I bet he could tell some doozies since the rest of his stories are."

"Don't you think it's big to be a person?"

"Some people have horrifically big feet. Could be that our bear has a little disfigurement too. It rather looks like it," he reconsidered with an awkward laugh. "It looks like both."

I took his word for it and was nodding when the frown returned to my face, "But you said a bear would have done more damage than that?"

With wrist balancing scratching fingers and the brim of his hat, Ketchum went at his hairline aggressively until a sigh dropped both hands limply to his sides.

"So I did," he agreed. "So I did."

CHAPTER FOUR

I developed the film at home, in the basement where I'd converted a root cellar into a darkroom. Years and years back I'd become paranoid that pictures I'd take would be ripped off or that somehow the developer could steal my whole story just by seeing a few pictures that had a lot of significance to me, but maybe nobody else. During that term of ambition driven paranoia, more than just pictures, I developed a love of photography and the art of chemically giving birth to photographs.

Rose-Marie just brought me lunch and she was thumbing through my notes and looking at the still dripping images of where I'd spent my time away from her. She wasn't jealous.

"So, what do you hear?" I asked the one person I knew who could get the scoop faster than me.

"Some of the campers from up there had to spend

the night at a motel in town and they said it sounded like Doug was losing his mind and carrying on while they heard the family screaming."

"Great."

Rose-Marie's umber colored eyes widened with some surprise and demurred, "I thought we hated that man."

"We're not friends, Rosie," I explained. "But the thing is that it was probably a bear. I talked to a ranger who said they already had a whole mess of reports about a bear up there that's probably diseased and too sick to be afraid of people and mean because it's sick."

"When are you going to let the rest of the world know?"

"I'm working on the article right now and by the time it comes out can I count on all this being no surprise to anyone?" I leaned back in my office chair to accept the kiss coming toward me.

"Why?"

"Because I need time to look into this some more and it would just really help a lot if this is what people thought, for now."

"What're *you* thinking about, Pat?" a hip much wider and softer than I'd known forty years ago rested up against the edge of my small desk. I tentatively raised my eyes to her face. There are times when I'd rather she didn't know me so well.

"I'm not sure," I deflected, even though she'd know there was at least something solid that made me "not sure".

Then she waited silently for me to tell her.

"There are some things that might implicate

something other than a bear or someone other than Napier. I believe Doug Napier is a worthless wino and lord knows he's a violent man, but more than one person put his hands on June Napier."

Rosie asked why I thought that and I told her:

"I saw the photos from Hill's coroner report. There were bruises on them that couldn't have been but from someone putting their hands on that family. Now I don't remember seeing anything like them on Napier, but I do remember a blatant inconsistency in Hill's photos."

Rosie took a breath and waited.

"There's some fella out there with hands like this," and I held them as far apart as I thought was reasonable, maybe fifty-percent more length of hand than I have, "because whoever this guy was choked June Napier and his fingers almost overlapped."

Then my wife cursed under her breath, rubbing thoughtfully at her own neck and looked me in the eyes.

"What're you thinking?"

I considered for a moment, not really sure until it was coming out of my mouth, "That park isn't very big, in the realm of things, but you could shit on the edge of it and smell the stink in the hundreds and hundreds of thousands of acres of National Forest practically just across the road."

I hesitated before finally telling her what she really wanted to know.

"I think there's some recluse up there in all those wild acres and he's a son-of-a-bitch."

Rose-Marie's expression reminded me that she didn't like me throwing the strong swears, but wasn't asking for an apology for that one.

"Have you looked at Doug's hands?" she wanted to know. I hadn't paid attention to them, that's for sure, but I think I would have noticed had they been that big, or the fingers that long. All I recalled was that they were still stained with blood. I was hoping to get a second chance when Hoffman would call about law enforcement finally getting a report from Napier. I'm no scientist, biologist or mathematician either, but I didn't think it would take much to eyeball some comparisons, take some notes and then some measurements on the copies of Hill's pictures. The ones I was going to call him for when I turned in my article about the bear attack to the boss.

*   *   *

I don't think I need to tell you how disappointed I was in George Hill when, after long talk and small talk, he came to the conclusion that it would be wrong to make copies of those pictures for me. I steeled myself against the bad news, telling myself that the police would have their own copies and ol' Chuck had never let me down. I wanted to say to Hill in my best Vincent Price, "It's only a matter of time."

Chuck had already come through for me once that night, calling just before supper that the doctors said Napier would be well enough for the interview the next day.

But this intermission of good news was surrounded by phone calls from people wanting to know if I knew anything. Chuck said he was getting asked about it too. Everybody seemed to know about the murders, but it doesn't take long to pass the word around a little more than one hundred people. People were scared, he said. He also said there were a lot of people confident that they already caught the killer and he was on the mend in Connolly. The word of a bear's involvement would force kids in from playing outside when the sun started going down—have dogs tied outside instead of let in overnight and already, it sounded like, a lot of people were thinking it a good idea to have weapons close by.

What I didn't like was how many of the callers, or people stopping Chuck on the street were asking if it really was Bigfoot and claiming to have had experiences of their own. One man told my wife, he knew it was only a matter of time before something like this happened.

The boss liked the article, he always did—like he knew enough about writing to even have an opinion—but he pressured me to write the Sasquatch angle he'd caught wind of. Apparently, once someone spilled the beans about what Napier was saying was responsible, a lot of people were coming forward with their own strange encounters and inundating the police with reports. My boss said it was "sensational" and leaned pretty hard until I pointed out to him what that would mean to our little town. He said the tourism might be good for the economy. I told him that I hoped he was joking.

The other boss made my favorite summer meal, cold chicken salad sandwiches, carrot and raisin salad, cinnamon rice and grape Kool-Aid, which the grandkids got me addicted to. There were only six flavors in the old days I liked them all and many of the varieties since, but I didn't go out of my way for any but grape. You tell me why.

I was a little anxious about seeing Doug again. I didn't know what the setup would be, I don't even know if the station was sat up for interrogations or anything. I thought maybe it would scare Napier into talking more, if he saw me, because he might think—oh damn, that was a cop and I was already so uncooperative. I better make up for it now.

Will see.

CHAPTER FIVE

"What do you mean you can't get me in?" I was yelling into the phone at Charlie Hoffman, while Rose-Marie tried to give full attention to my conversation and making breakfast.

"I'm sorry, Stephen, Sheriff Krantz says absolutely not."

"Can I talk to him?"

"He was mad that I even asked, man. He says it's unethical. But I think he just doesn't trust that you're not gonna go run off and work your career with this. People are getting pretty excited about this and we need to avoid anything that's going to provoke hysteria—like speculation. There was nothing I could do to change his mind," Chuck sounded sincerely apologetic and I almost appreciated it. I would have, if I had gotten my way, but since I didn't I was pretty much pissed at everyone.

"Who can I talk to? This is really important to me," which was a lie, because I was still holding a grudge against my boss for waking me up for this story, even though it was maybe getting a little more interesting to me than it was for most of first day on it.

"Listen, Stephen, I am pretty sure I can get you a copy of the tapes when I make one for transcription."

That was better than nothing, but barely.

"Who's transcribing it?" I probed, feeling a smile blooming on my mouth. My wife noticed it too and raised an eyebrow at my sudden change of tone.

"Probably Janet Burns. Never had to have that before."

"Look, Charlie, you don't want a secretary sitting on that kind of information—" I could feel the protest rising in the silence on the other end of the line, about to tell me what a good person she was "—I know you trust her, but this is sensitive stuff and while well meaning, she's young and might not know how to keep things confidential like she should. If you think you could get me a copy, why don't you just let me do the transcription? I can type like a hummingbird flies and besides…"

I paused until Ol' Chuck was just about dying with anticipation, saying, "What? What?!"

"…I think I've stumbled on some things that are going to change everything you thought you knew was happening in this case. You're going to want me to do the transcription. The fewer people who know, the better. Trust me."

"I do. Alright, Patterson. I'll work it out."

Of course I do, I thought confidently, that's what I wanted. Then I had to know:

"When's the interview?"

"Umm. Will be after supper, sometime. The doctor thinks Doug will be less anxious on a full stomach."

"Will it be good for his stomach to be full if he has to talk about this crap?"

"Seriously, Patterson?" I wasn't used to Chuck talking to me like *I* wasn't thinking. "On an empty stomach a body feels like they're nauseous even when they're not and if he's one to get all shaky if his blood sugar gets low we'll get nowhere."

Chuck was right and I didn't like that (I was such a prick). Not that I couldn't use it to my advantage, I told him, "That's why I go to you. You got New York City instincts in Mayberry demands."

Hoffman offered his pleased, "Ayuh." I remember thinking at the time the weird sounds his wife might hear in bed.

"So what do you think you've found?"

To that I thought, *Don't you mean, 'What did you find?' What do I THINK I found?*

"…patronize me…," I was mumbling.

"Sorry? Missed that," Chucky said loudly like I was the one who didn't hear him.

"Can we meet somewhere?"

He said, "Sure," and we decided where and when.

"Do you have access to any of the crime scene photos?"

"What d'you mean? There are like two deputies even looking at this, not counting the sheriff. Of course, I have access to them."

"Then I need you to bring them."

The silence on the other end of the line showed a hesitation I didn't like in Chuck. He *never* doubted me.

"I thought you said you trust me," I didn't try to hide my annoyance, was time to put the boy back in his place.

"It's not that. Do you really want to see them?"

I grunted loudly, and guffawed for just the right touch of bemusement, then I almost called him "Chuck", "Ch-arlie, you know I was already up at Hill's. I saw everything. The only reason I'm asking is that I don't have pictures of some of the injuries I want to talk to you about and I don't think Hill will provide them to be props."

Hoffman then agreed to bring what he had. I didn't tell him anything specific so he would do just that. I was craving information and letting what I perceived to be "the facts" fit together in my mind.

"One more thing Hoffman."

He answered with a normal, "Yeah."

"How many people do you think are living under the radar out in the wilderness around here?"

"Do you mean anti-government hippy—"

"I mean like 'backwoods' folks, separatists."

"I couldn't say, Stephen. I don't have much call to know where people go home to when I see them around and don't get around to a lot of people's places, except people I'm closer to."

"So, conceivably, we could have some hermits and the like roughing it in unsettled patches," I always added "hick" talk in when I was trying to meet Chuck on a local level.

"I'm sure there are," Chuck sounded pretty certain of this. So I thanked him and hung up.

"So you're not going to get to be there?" my wife poo-pooed. I'm not sure if she was offering pity or teasing me. I was too distracted to care. My mind was reeling. I had a feeling that Hoffman's pictures would settle the mystery once and for all. I don't know why this was, but I felt like I would crack the case once I got a look at them. I already felt, if you remember, that I knew more than all of the police around here put together. It would upholster my ego to do what they couldn't, that was catch a killer. They caught an S.O.B. That's all. I knew it. Pretty soon they'd know it too.

I had time to kill, but I ate like I didn't. In between bites I asked her what she thought about the idea of a disfigured wild man or survivalist being responsible.

"It would feel a lot better on the community if the deed belonged to someone no one knew."

"Do you know any of Napier's in-laws?"

"I know the family," Rosie said. I figured she would. Chuck Hoffman might not get around to know everybody and where they live, but my sweet bride was a social butterfly, always had been.

"Have you ever seen them? June was blonde as straw, but her brother—"

"The red-head? I think those Dyer's are every shade between blond and crimson. Must be Irish?"

"I think they're Scandinavian," I guessed without having a clue.

My wife shrugged.

"Do you think this could belong to any one of them?" I asked her. I was struck with a bothered feeling I couldn't straighten out into one feeling or another. It was bothering me that my wife knew people, was about to tell me she *did know* what they looked like pretty well, and they could be *murderers*…brutal homicidal murderers. Like finding out after sixty years that she'd kissed somebody before we were dating and getting pissed at her. I didn't like that my wife could have been around people who could do what I saw done.

"It definitely could be, Pat, but how many red-heads do you think are around here?"

I shrugged, like anyone smart would have. There was no way to know, but there were redheads in the family and crimes like this were almost always family. Really fucking pissed off family. And, depending on their histories, they might have had a lot to be pissed off about, but why they would take it out on anyone but Napier himself was beyond me, but I didn't think it was going to be all that challenging to come up with an answer.

*   *   *

I met up with Charlie Hoffman around ten o'clock, Friday, August 5th. We agreed to meet at his place because no one would pay any attention and his wife was working until 4:30, so talking freely wouldn't be a problem.

It was hard for me to believe the last two days—time went so fast, I felt like I always had a million things to do. Sitting there, sipping intensely strong black coffee, a feeling of non-reality washed over me. I felt like I must be dreaming, like that moment in a dream that seems all too real where something weird happens and you realize it can't *really* be happening? This weird thing couldn't really be happening to us, I felt. I was about to go over photos of murder victims with a police officer and let him know that, while Doug looked good for some of the bruises, he wasn't the only one that hurt that woman and children.

And when I was done with telling him what I first noticed, at Hills, that the hands involved were two different sizes, about the red-brown hair clenched in June Napier's fist, about the foot print and everything the ranger told me up there. Chuck Hoffman looked up at me with those large, simple looking eyes and asked, "Where's the hair?"

I didn't miss a beat and answered, "It's up at George Hill's. He got it out of June's hand," but underneath I cursed him out.

"We're going to have to take a look at that. Send it to the crime lab in Seattle, maybe."

"Do you think it's enough to get a warrant on the brother-in-law?"

Chuck shrugged, "I doubt it. Besides, if he was responsible and there's nothing wrong with his feet, the judge would just let him walk away. He won't be troubled by our troubles unless we have more than similar hair."

I slapped my forehead hard, too hard, but something just dawned on me that pushed past the foolishly earned pain.

"It's not the brother."

"Why do you say that now?"

"I saw him at the hospital—he was fine—if he'd been into it with Napier he'd have been messed up. Doug couldn't have earned his reputation for being mean by being a pipsqueak, someone would have kicked his ass into place by now. If he had tangled with Napier, it would have shown."

We talked a little about what the crime lab could tell us and back then it wasn't a lot. It would be two more years until DNA testing was available.

"You're really observant, you know," Chuck commented as he went back over his notes of what I'd brought up.

"I wish I had more time with yours or Hill's photos—all of that is just the stuff I noticed on fairly quick once through."

"You know those are copies for you, don't you?" Hoffman sounded incredulous.

"How would I know that?"

"We are conducting a possible murder investigation. I had to make copies so nobody would miss them. So you might as well have them."

I thanked him, sincerely.

"You've helped, Stephen. I see that as helping us both. Oh crap—I just had an—"

"What?" I wondered as he hurriedly moved for his light coat and hat.

"The print!"

Chuck thought he'd have time to run over to the park and back before the interview. He wanted to make a plaster cast of the footprint if it was still there, but he needed to stop over in Connolly because he thought the Ben Franklin might carry plaster-of-Paris.

"So what do I tell the others?" he sounded nervous.

"It all depends on what Napier says."

"You think there's a good chance that there's some diseased bear or lunatic out there might have done this?"

I nodded.

"Then we're gonna have to get out there and track him down before he does this again."

"Don't get ahead of yourself," I warned. Chuck was about to protest.

"You haven't even heard what Napier has to say."

The following chapter is based on transcripts taken of the police interview with Doug Napier, tape recorded 7:10pm Friday, August 5th, 1983. The questioning was conducted by deputies Charlie Hoffman and David Schaller. County Sheriff John Krantz listened and supervised from another room.

CHAPTER SIX

"It wasn't all that bright out, the moon was only about a third full and we'd put the fire out even though the area was mostly dirt by the ring and we could still see the lights of other fires through the trees where we hadn't heard talking in the longest while so we all assumed they'd went on to bed without bothering. The kids were enamored with it, having been the first they'd helped with. I think they liked to see how long...," only the sound of hard swallowing followed for moments, "...how long it'd last."

"It was nearly morning, why didn't you let them have their way?"

"Why do you think?"

"Man, I have no idea."

Napier leaned back in his chair, rubbing his jaw. The stubble of several days without shaving made a dry sound in the small interview room. His left hand, which hadn't left the arm of the chair since he first sat in it, constricted on the padded vinyl which creaked in protest of the white-knuckled grip.

"So what happened next?"

The muscles under those four or five days of stubble rippled as Napier clenched his teeth. The line I had seen repeatedly at the hospital returned to the space between his deeply frowning eyes.

"I was laying on my face, sleeping, when I was woked by something reeking worse than a dirty dogs old blanket. I've never smelled something like that in the whole of my life. It was something like pigsty and human stink. Maybe I can't describe it, cuz there's nothing else like it. Anyway, it was enough to rouse me and when I raised up on my elbow and my head outta the pillow I could hear something moving around out there. I checked—" he made a wheezing sound and put his right hand over his face like the sun was in his eyes "—checked on my wife, Juh—" a high short sound squeezed out of his pressed lips. One of the deputies told him to take his time, after a few breaths Napier tried again.

"She wasn't sleeping, even as she was laying there. I knew she was listening to it too."

"Are you sure?" Schaller asked.

"Does it matter? Yes I'm sure. I knew. You always know, don't ya? A body can tell if someone's awake or no, especially if you been sleeping beside—beside them for ten year."

"Okay, she's awake. Then what?"

"Then...then I heard it snuff and sniff once or twice. Then it was coming through the tent...

The baby felt so small, Doug almost thought he'd left half of James behind when he snatched the three-year-old off the tent floor. He was vaguely aware of June grabbing up their daughter while he hooked his arm around their oldest and threw himself through the opening the intruder just made. He was pushing the kids into his wife's child-filled arms when behind them, their second oldest, Randy, made a bleating sound cut short by the horrible wet thump of a rotten pumpkin being thrown against pavement.

June's screams drowned out his own.

There was no thought to arming himself, the urgency allowed for little thought at all—Randy was the only one of the four children not crying—the silence filled him with a peerless level of dread and loathing. All he could think to do was punch it, even though what he really wanted to do was rip it into pieces. When his fists found purchase in the invader, they sunk into a firmly muscled mass covered in long hair. It turned to respond to the attacks and Doug found that the bear he assumed he was punching, was narrow and he could feel the skeleton underneath the sinewy muscle, like punching a very tall, very hairy athlete. He'd used those fists a hell of a lot of times in his life, never once on any beast—even so, it didn't feel right. Not even if the bear was starving and there'd be no reason for that.

The realization gave him pause, but only that. All at once he felt and smelled its pungent, sauna-like breath on his face, felt his wife's small body pushing past him and the force of a log-like forearm driving against his chest, then his body driven against the pebbly grass-less earth near the fire-ring.

In the dark, June was screaming. The footsteps racing past could have only belonged to their oldest, Dennis.

Doug yelled for them to get away from it, picking himself off the ground.

The thing had its back to him. Without seeing it, it was obvious to Doug that he couldn't pull it off them. The next thing he knew, one of the blackened logs from the fire was in his hands and he laid into the hairy thing with strength and speed that registered as foreign to his consciousness, as he heard the crunch of the burnt outside breaking away from the healthy internal meat of the log, into the meat of the animal.

It roared in pain and surprise and, Doug thought, rage.

Someone's fingers were trying to get ahold of the folds at the knees of his jeans and he stooped to grab the arm attached to them and yank whoever it was away. June cried out in surprise and he knew the hold he took was harder than he meant.

"Get the kids!" he hurried.

"The keys—"

"Just run!" he yelled severely while probing the darkness for any part of either child.

He felt smallish hands find his back and knew their fifteen-year-old was there. At almost the same time he found Randy's upper leg, he'd wore shorts and his favorite t-shirt for pajamas. His hand followed the leg until it rested on the chest that, in the dark, felt no bigger than it had six years before, when Randy was only one. No one had to tell Doug Napier if someone was breathing or not, any more than he needed someone to tell him what blood feels like when you can't see it—or what it smells like for that matter. The thirty-nine-year-old could find a pulse if he had to do it without fingers—he depressed the soft flesh under what seemed like an impossibly small mandible. A stillness waited there that he immediately refused, even as he knew and expected it.

What he did not expect, when he instinctively, paternally reached to touch that little face was that there was none to be found.

In these mere seconds since he'd told June to run, he heard the escalating breath of a man building up a cry. The howl that shredded the darkness was like the driving wind of a tornado decimating the air next to an ear.

While its mouth was still agape, while the sound was still raping the peace from the dwindling night, a flashlight came alive and struck the rounded crest, low brow and the bared white teeth framing what, in the contrast of light and dark, looked like a very deep mouth.

Dennis shrieked and, like his father earlier, was flung to the ground.

A long, massive hand seized Doug by his left arm and yanked him off the ground. The sound of the arm bone breaking resounded next to his ear. His right fist drove into the wide-flat nose, then the side of its head when it turned, then drove without thinking into the upper lip, the exposed gums and grated away plenty of skin and flesh on the teeth.

The light dropped to a height he knew belonged to their daughter. Then June was at its back, her straw-blonde hair, Doug would think, looking back, seemed especially golden and shiny in that single beam of light. Her eyes, in their fear widened state, shining with tears, were more beautiful than he ever remembered. The color on her cheeks had never been higher, from the worst he'd ever seen her sunburned, to the flush of their most intense lovemaking. June looked right into her husband's face the split second before the creature grabbed her throat and began to squeeze it.

In the light of the flashlight he saw her slender hands make fists into its long hair.

His torn right hand was delivering a fifth hit when, while holding the detached end of Doug's broken right arm, the thing tossed him aside, against what was still standing of the tent.

The light from the flashlight bounced as the user started running away.

Doug heard the heavy pounding of the thing's feet as it crashed through the remains of the campfire, across the dirt and into the pine needle and grass carpeted woods. He heard his six-year-old daughter make a sound like a hiccup. He heard the "FWOP!" of something fleshy ricochet across the dirt of their camping lot. James was crying and Dennis was making a wet wheezing sound...no one needed to tell Doug what that meant either.

The thing was berserk when it returned to the camp. It was tearing things apart. It was tearing everything apart. Doug was losing consciousness as the creature started back to him and was only vaguely aware when it first put its nails into his skin…

There it seemed like the interview might have ended. The silence thereafter lasted so long I was just about to shut off the tape when Schaller said:

"You said earlier you hadn't been drinking."

"No..." Napier sniveled into the hands cupping his face.

"You and June use any drugs of any kind?"

"Not since I got back."

"Got back?" Schaller was dubious.

"From overseas?" Hoffman offered.

Napier nodded into his palms; the hair at his forehead stood on end where his fingertips divided it.

"Some of you fellas come back and you can't make sense of things, of normal life anymore..." Schaller began, easing into the chair next to him, like he was about to comfort a friend. Napier was still, with his brow leaned into his hands, so still it was like he stopped breathing. Maybe for the moment he had.

"...and sometimes you boys have such a hard time that life becomes unbearable and they snuff themselves out..."

Barely noticeable, Napier's chin tilted toward the deputy.

"...and there are times that you boys are so lost and hurt and mad that you go mad and sometimes they hurt people they don't mean to."

The slight tilt dropped the almost unmeasureable distance back to where it was.

"I didn't hurt my family."

"But you've hurt them before, haven't you?"

Napier's shoulder's twitched.

"You've hurt a lot of people and we understand all that and what you been through. We understand you made a mistake."

"What you're saying is you weren't able to find the bear," Doug dropped the hand between his face and looking at David. "You weren't able to find the bear because there wasn't no goddamn fucking bear!"

Napier's chair flipped over when he stood and moved to pace in the corner.

"There was a bear," Hoffman insisted.

"NNNO!" the rumpled man screamed so hard he folded in on himself to push out all the air.

"It-was-no-bear!" he repeated, stabbing his finger at them with each word.

"Come on, sid-down Doug," Hoffman tried to calm him. "You know we need to look at this thing from all angles. You want us to consider everything, for their sake, right?"

Charlie gestured for the other deputy to give Doug some space and move back to the other side of the table.

"But you're not," Napier pointed tiredly. He picked up the chair and lowered himself into it slowly, his body was hurting pretty good after that.

"A sasquatch is a little hard to swallow," Hoffman returned.

"I never said it was a squatch," the shredded man firmly reminded. "I just told you what I saw. I didn't call it any fuckin' thing. I wouldn't even know what to call it."

"Do you believe in Bigfoot?" David probed.

Napier's eyes drifted up to Deputy Schaller's, "There are some things we believe in without any proof, because we got a need to—that's asking a lot of any body, but we think what we gotta think, often to make life just a little easier. I ain't never had any proof before of them, ain't never had no need to believe in them. If a squatch is what that was, then they are real, regardless of what I believe. If it wasn't, then it's some other thing—one big fuckin' problem."

"Do you think you hurt it?" Hoffman wondered.

"It sounded like it got hurt," Napier remembered.

"Hadn't you been warned about a bear coming up on campers? Don't you think that fire might have kept it out of your camp that night?" Schaller inquired.

"It wasn't no bear. Jesus Christ, I'd know a bear if all I had to go on was the smell of it, I'd know it, but I got a lot more than just smell to tell it by. I heard it. I seen it. I touched it!"

"It was a bear—"

"It wasn't no bear," the disheveled man spat against the foam capsuled microphone. "Bear don't have people teeth."

A chill rushed through Hoffman's flesh, like being goosed by Jack Frost.

David Schaller stumbled over an automatic answer and forgot what he was thinking, he only knew he didn't like what he just heard or the tone of how he heard it. This man wasn't itching for attention, he wasn't excited about something "bizarre" that happened to him. If any other man had been sitting there, he told me later, he'd have believed him, but he didn't really think Doug Napier was sober enough to remember what to remember.

"Did you know Mrs. Whitton came to see you at the hospital," Charlie opted to change the subject. "She said you'd been attending church over in the next town almost every weekend since your youngest was baptized there."

"It's closer to our place," Napier mumbled tiredly.

"I bet that's helped a lot since you got out of service."

"I was drafted," the answer fell flatly from Napier's mouth.

"Sorry. Has it helped?"

"I had a lot to work through. June…said it might."

"I'd say that's a sign of good character," Charlie's voice was soft and calming. A hitching sob came from behind Napier's raised hands. It took him almost a minute and a half before he could answer:

"It has nothing to do with being good," his voice was husky with emotion. "But my missus said if I was brave enough to face my peers with my wrongs that I could face myself. I could turn my life around."

"Did you?" Schaller leaned back, folding his arms across his chest.

"No," Napier said definitely. He rubbed his eyes and face with an open hand before dropping it at his side. "I talked to that preacher man and he told us that there ain't no such thing. That would mean changing the past and you cain't. You can only go forward and do what you can with each day."

"Did you?" this time Hoffman asked.

Napier's head swiveled limply and didn't actually come to face Charlie.

"When I came back first baby wasn't no baby anymore. Then the next 'uns came, I wasn't there for them and when I was there, I think they wished I wasn't. One night I was on a bender and I took June by her wrists in one hand and made to smack her good with the other when she cried out, 'Don't hurt the baby!' My world stood still, then it was full of crying kids, crying wife. Broken things, broken home. Frightened eyes…and they was all on me, because of me. Why I saw it then, instead of all the other times? I suppose it was because of what she said. That's not the kind of thing a normal person would ever hear. Maybe that made me realize that I didn't know me. The unborn child was James. I—I made—" his face screwed up to keep the tears down. After a perfectly quiet moment, he finished "—I made every promise of myself around that baby, like it was my reincarnation or something. But I suppose, in a way it was. My daddy was a mean son-of-a-bitch and no matter how I hetted him, I became one too because we share the same life. The same space. Just like my son and I would. I was already reliving my wrong life in the three I already born. He was like every promise…"

Then he drifted off.

"I'm sorry Doug," Deputy Schaller said in a different tone than he'd yet used—a compassionate one. "I am sorry about what happened. Now I don't think you're lying about what you saw up there, but I do know that fear and darkness do no favors to a man's sense or reality. I do think there's a bear up there that we're gonna shoot here, real soon, and it's going to be sick and out of its mind with being sick and it's going to have blood on it and you're going to see how in the dark you might have mistaken it for something unnatural—let me tell you something, I've seen what some of these parasites can do to a body and they don't look like anything you ever saw."

"It's true," Charlie agreed. "I talked to one of the rangers up there just today and they've seen animals with the mange that makes them look like they crawled out of hell and not hibernation, if you get what I mean."

"But I've seen sick animals. I've seen mange..." Napier said, barely audibly.

"But you were really scared, weren't you?" David Schaller gently reminded.

"More than I've ever been," Napier agreed stiffly— like he was remembering his worst fears to confirm this as true.

"We're going to release you back to the hospital now. It sounds like another week and you'll be able to go home. The reason why Mrs. Whitton came calling on you was wanting to know if she could come fetch you for church this Sunday," Hoffman told him. "I told her you probably wouldn't be up for that."

"I'm not," Napier agreed, again, almost too quietly for the microphone to pick up. And then, without barely opening his teeth or lips, "When can I make arrangements for my family?"

"I'll call Hill's tonight."

"George Hill?" Napier asked Hoffman clearly.

"Yep."

"No," Napier said firmly. "That sumbitch tried to overcharge Fred Crew when his daddy passed. Got the charges itemized and had all kinds of services they didn't ask for and didn't get. Preying on folks that are already hurting? Fuck him."

"Well you know your options are few," Schaller reminded. In fact, he couldn't even think of another funeral home reasonably close.

"I'll call Jerry Jacobs," a local carpenter and woodworker who had once, when pulled over for possibly driving intoxicated, defended himself by informing the officer that he didn't drink, although he'd love to, because he works with too dangerous of tools. He had, in fact, been swerving because he'd just pulled a double shift at the mill and was running on about two hours of sleep.

Napier considered a moment and added, "The preacher up there, I think, will do a fine service—at least he'll know who he's talking about."

"We'll make sure you get a hold of whoever you need to," Hoffman promised.

Napier's "Thanks." was inaudible, but Chuck told me he heard it.

*   *   *

Because Napier entering Connelly's police station might cause undue conjecture, the powers that be (Schaller and Krantz) agreed the remote community center—serving the three small towns, mostly as a dance and meeting hall—was a wiser venue to host the interview.

The deputies waited on the steps until the hospital van was out of sight. Schaller went for a cigarette and Chuck bummed one.

"Jee-sus," Deputy Schaller grunted.

"What do you think?" Hoffman probed.

"I think he thinks he's telling the truth. My guess is he's not a good liar."

"Why do you say that?" Chuck wondered.

"He doesn't have the self-control. He has been shitting all across this world for thirty-nine years and never looked down to see what he was shitting on. He's a creature of habit and he's indulgent. He's admitted he's just three years into the baby steps of learning restraint. You have to know how to censor yourself to lie. I don't think he knows how. Shit—he's too fucking scrambled right now anyway."

"Napier's right about one thing, bear or no, it's going to be a problem. Most animals when they've killed a person they won't be shy to attack a second time. If it's got a taste for blood..."

"It's a bear, Hoffman," Schaller retorted.

"What's the difference? People have been seeing these things all over the country. There are pictures, casts, video and making recordings of the sounds they make."

"You been looking into this?"

"I wasn't bullshitting when I said I was going to look at this from all angles. Suppose we got something up here—one of those things. Word gets out and we'll have the whole country up our asses over it—especially with five deaths. We're going to have to hire someone and hire someone good. I've been saying since day one that we need a hunter."

"Well I could get a whole volunteer party of—"

"No!" Hoffman cut him off. "No. We don't need this in any more ears than need to hear it. We have to make this thing go away, the sooner the better."

"Can you find the man?" Schaller asked doubtfully.

"I'll ask around, maybe get the word out about the sick bear."

"Word's already out. Didn't you see the paper?"

"Well then, we'll get the word out that we're looking for a hunter to track it down."

"If you want to keep this quiet, I think we need to tell people the bear's done been shot and that nobody can go into that fucking park until the rangers say it's safe, since there might be more sick animals. Then nobody will be looking or thinking about it except us and the Joe we get to get in there after it. You spread the word around a place like this that we need a few good men to go after a murdering bear??? We'll get mad riflemen showing up from Canton."

"That makes sense. So how do we find someone?"

"Maybe we start asking around. Ask people who they think shot the bear. Maybe that the fella laid it out in one long shot. Tell them we heard he was a damn good hunter and see who they think fits the bill."

Charlie Hoffman lit up like a Christmas tree, praising, "That's really clever, David. Where'd you learn to think like that?"

"I didn't just put on the uniform to become a cop," Schaller sounded a little irritated, but since most the time when he talked it sounded like he didn't really want to, it was hard to say for certain.

"When these Sasquatch have been hunted before, people have gone out with huge parties—do you think it's safe—"

"I'm a little surprised you're taking this seriously," David criticized.

"I never would have before," Hoffman explained helplessly, "but this guy I know pointed out some things to me that are hard not to take seriously. Things Napier here just corroborated in his account of that night."

"Are you going to tell me?" Deputy Schaller urged as Hoffman started off toward his patrol car.

"When we find the hunter, I'll bring that guy and show you, Krantz and him both. Then the five of us can maybe sort this out."

"It better be good, Charlie," David warned half-seriously and dropped behind the wheel of his own car.

The other deputy peeled out of the parking lot, leaving Charlie Hoffman alone in the off colored light of dusk. The bronze keys flipped over and over themselves, so distracted he'd already flipped past the car keys twice. Finding the right set, he finally looked up to the way Schaller left, only he was looking at the silhouetted wilderness beyond the road. It was no longer reliable, understandable. Hoffman knew damn well there were dangerous things out there; there are dangerous things everywhere. But now it was something untrustworthy, keeping secrets—he felt like it'd lied to him all his life. Hoffman no longer knew what things were out there at all.

"You won't believe it," Charlie finally, quietly answered.

CHAPTER SEVEN

Hoffman came over right after the interview and played the tape for me. I was about to go through the hardest thing I could remember having to up until then. When I thought I'd have all the pieces of the puzzle, this was not what I had in mind. Going to George Hill was like going to a casting party. I got to meet all the actors and find out what happened to them in the story. I'd been to the set, the ranger walked me through who was where and whatever he could piece together about the in-betweens. Now, in my mind, the bloody patches of ground were covered in the bodies removed from them. When I listened to the tape, it was like the director yelled, "ACTION!"

The pieces did fall into place. The reason for the bruises on the kids and Mrs. Napier were explained. Napier's broken arm. The skin under June's nails and how much hair she'd ripped out and the terrible struggle that led to both.

By this point, I need to tell you, I was scared. I was scared of what we were dealing with, but more scared because there were some big doubts about what that meant exactly.

Since nobody knew or knows what a Sasquatch is—for all I knew, talking about a mutated wild man might have been one in the same thing. After all, many of the American Indian terms for Sasquatch mean "hairy men", although my wife pointed out to me that no monkeys inhabit the United States naturally—they couldn't actually describe them as ape-like, could they, she said. But I was beginning to think that we really were just talking about people. Our version of *The Hills Have Eyes*' people.

In 1840 Reverend Elkanah Walker recorded stories of giants living among the natives near Spokane. They lived high up in the mountains and stole fish from them.

In the 1920's, Indian Agent J.W. Burns recounted stories from the Sts'Ailes people where these wild men were known to speak.

Around the same time, in British Columbia, Elizabeth Wallace reported being kidnapped and held prisoner by a large hairy "man", for lack of a better word.

In 1924, Fred Beck and four other Washington miners were attacked in their cabin the same year that a British Columbian prospector, Albert Ostman, was also held captive by a "creature".

A third of all Sasquatch or Bigfoot sightings are in the Pacific Northwest. There are lots and lots incidents that seem more like people to me than animals.

Maybe there's some kind of human race we've never seen. Maybe there are Bigfoot, if there are, what are they? Are they an alternative to the little green men from space? Some people think so. Some people also attribute Sasquatch to supernatural beings, mostly demonic. Based on what happened up at Lot 9, I think it could only be that…or a human.

The only thing left to do was ask an expert.

Only I didn't know any.

That was when Chuck suggested I meet Jeffrey Green.

CHAPTER EIGHT

Jeffrey Green lived up one of the longest and prettiest drives west of Pennsylvania. Like Doug Napier, he was drafted to serve in Nam. When he got back from the war, he officially gave up teaching science at one of Okanogan County's largest high schools and went into mining. Folks said that he lasted one day back in the classroom, but there was something about it he just couldn't do. Something about mining fit him right because he'd been doing it ever since.

Chuck Hoffman didn't know anyone else around here who might have answers. We agreed that the hunter should know if he was looking for a man, a bear, or a giant bipedal ape before setting out to hunt it or else who knows what might be killed.

Unlike the drive up, Green's home wasn't as welcoming. I don't really know what I was expecting—a Dutch Colonial?

The cabin at the end of the driveway had seen better days, unless it was purposefully rustic. The timbers were graying, there were a couple places where the boards on the porch and stairs already gave and the corrugated metal roofing was rusty and patched. This was the kind of place, without being posted, said "No Trespassing".

There was no answer to my knocks, but when I gave up I heard what turned out to be purposefully loud clanging and banging from the back.

The driveway swung around the cabin and doing so sloped downward to a garage below the main building. The man was donned in camo pants, a white t-shirt, and a sweat stained Yankees baseball cap.

"I figured if it was important you'd come around," came the disembodied voice of the man leaning deep under a truck's hood.

"Well I don't know how important it is…" might not have been the best way to begin the conversation.

The man leaned back to look at me, like there was a nice pair of legs drifting away on a busy city sidewalk. His wrist scratched at a trickle of sweat tickling its way down his neck. A rag came out of his back pocket and, in a way my wife despises, wiped his hands on the cloth, pretty much by balling it up, kneading it and stuffing it haphazard back where it came from. If his hands were any cleaner, I couldn't tell it, but I shook the hand when it was offered.

"I'm Stephen Patterson. I'm looking for Jeff Green."

"You found him, if you'll remember to call him Jeffrey," the man informed with a pleasant smile. "Are you the same Stephen Patterson who wrote that article about the bear attack?"

"That's actually why I'm here to see you."

Green looked surprised, a one-sided grin accompanied the "Why?" that followed.

"I just wanted to make sure it was a bear."

Jeffrey Green chuckled a little, he squinted his eyes like that would help him hear better what he just heard.

"You know bear are big, right?" the rhetoric was presented in a way that you might give it to a child, soft and obvious.

"Obviously."

"See!" and he pointed right at me, "That's the perfect word, 'obvious'. Well, when something big has been involved with anything, that's what it is. Wasn't there a ranger you could ask?"

"I talked to Paul Ketchum."

"Well, he's not an idiot?" Green sounded confused and I felt a little insulted.

"I'm glad you know him."

"I know him some," he'd returned to the engine. "We used to go fishing in the old days. We'd get messes of rough-fish together to give to girlfriends' parents."

I smiled to myself, instantly enjoying flashbacks of the things I did for love when I was young and poor.

"Some of the things we found at the camp, he wasn't sure about. I wanted a second opinion and there aren't a lot of people to go to."

"Who sent you to me?" was the first time he sounded dead serious.

"Charlie Hoffman," I answered, almost giving "Chuck" again.

"Okay."

That's all you have to say? I thought.

"So, what would Paul not know that I would?" I guess that meant that it was okay that Ol' Chuck sent me.

"There was a weird track and some behavior that he thought was strange for a bear."

"Like?"

"Like it just killing people, not eating, barely biting them. Have you ever known a bear to throw something it attacked? Because one of the victims was supposedly dragged out of the camp, based on the packed and bent grass, but there were no tracks. My guess was, the body was thrown."

"Do you know how many people went up to that, what are they? Fifteen by thirty feet lots? At most."

"We found a track that wasn't trampled. I got a good picture of it too and hopefully the cast will turn out."

"Paul wouldn't need me to identify any track," Jeffrey dismissed with a wave of his hand.

"I'm not just here for fun," I pressed firmly. "Why would I come all the way out here if Ketchum had known?"

He considered this.

"Okay, I'm listening."

"You mean you weren't before?" I asked.

Jeffrey's cobalt blue eyes, the only thing with definite color until you reached the trees, finally looked like they were looking at me and I knew I was going to get my answers and a little more than what I'd come for:

"I thought you were going to ask me to hunt it."

He said he just tuned me out, waiting for me to get to the point.

"You hunt bear?" I asked.

He answered, "I hunt everything."

Then I heard myself asking, "You ever hunted a sasquatch?"

He looked at me sideways. Then the one-sided grin reappeared.

"You ever hunt leprechauns?"

I laughed, maybe a little exaggeratedly, "Well you said you hunt everything."

"You can't hunt nothing," he replied, taking out the rod and dropping the hood.

"Sorry. I was just being a smartass," I felt like my excuse was solid.

"You don't have to be sorry—it was funny," only I think he purposefully sounded like it wasn't funny at all.

"If I show you what I need to ask you about, can I have your word that you won't talk about this with anyone? Hoffman said you're an honest man, so your word's good enough by me."

"Hoffman doesn't know me well enough to claim that, but thank him," Jeffrey Green answered in a relaxed way. "But you can't ask for my help and give me ultimatums. I'll help you if I can. Is that good enough?"

I agreed and followed him back to the front yard, assuming I was supposed to, since he never said he wasn't coming right back. He didn't invite me in, but offered me the rocking chair on the porch and he took the regular chair at the table, small enough to only hold a dinner plate and a beer.

I had a sudden urge to take my things and run to the station wagon before I shared my thoughts with another living soul. It was probably the journalist in me refusing to share information, but it might have been the part of me that was afraid of word getting out and this small, sparsely populated county—third largest in the continental United States—becoming a dive for desperate reporters, psychotic huntsmen, over-zealous thrill seekers, Bigfoot stalkers and herds of tourists charging through people's land wildly taking snapshots of moose and trying to sell them to tabloids. We didn't need that here. I wasn't going to let that happen here.

I handed over my files, including my photos, the crime scene photos and the transcript I'd written up, for myself and the police—these were all actually copies because I was afraid to bring the originals and have him decide to take them or something.

"To your questions about bear behavior," Jeffrey said in a distracted voice, but he was still looking through my information. "Bear don't always eat what they kill. Bear have huge claws, in case you didn't know, and don't rely on their teeth to do everything. Bear are perfectly capable of lifting things, they do it all the time. I don't know if they are capable of throwing or just dropping things, I'd have to look into it, but the mystery in that could easily be chalked up to the emergency services attending to that victim and destroying any evidence. What did the coroner say?"

"Bear attack."

"And Paul?"

"Bear attack."

"Witnesses?"

"Ketchum said there were a lot of complaints over the past weeks about a nuisance bear. The only survivor of the attack doesn't think it was a bear, but he was terrified."

"Douglas?" he said.

"Yeah, Doug Napier."

He nodded to himself and said nothing for a few seconds.

"And what do you think?" Green asked me.

"I think it was a man," the answer came out as simply as I felt it.

"So do I," he committed passively. "None of this is bear."

I wanted to know how he could be so definitively certain about something where other people were so sure of something else.

"Paul Ketchum didn't examine the bodies, did he?" he answered with a question—which I don't particularly like—unless I do it.

"No."

"The canvas wasn't shredded, it's ripped. A bear's claws wouldn't have done that—that looks like something tore through it, not clawed through. Bear are fast, but this would have to be fast and agile to chase down six people, without any of them getting away. That's speculation because we don't know all the factors, like how long the attack took, if people ran, when? How fast could they move? I think it's reasonable to think that a bear that would do this wouldn't have ignored the other campers within smelling distance—" I told him what Ketchum said about it maybe being bothered by the loud sound of arguing. Which some witness said they heard, others swore they hadn't. To which Jeffrey shrugged, and made a point about diseased animals from a book that, ironically, would be released in movie theaters in just seven days. "This isn't *Cujo*. No animal is going to kill all these people because they are being loud. It might get aggressive with one or two people if the sound was threatening, but not six, even if it was out of its mind."

"What else?"

"A bear doesn't strangle things. Bear don't have long fingers. Bear do have claws, but they would cut deeper than this. Most of these wounds, on their own, are superficial. It's not unrealistic to think that an animal isn't going to get in their best hit every time, but when you consider the force behind a bear, the claws and how sharp they are, make this look more like a bear accidently scratching someone a lot. These scratches are more like gouges than slices—you can tell by the shape of the wound—like human scratches. All the scratches look bad and were definitely a contributing factor, but these people were essentially beaten to death. A tool or tools were used. This was a person."

"Any idea what kind of man we're looking at?" he was on a roll, I figured I'd let him keep batting.

"Between twenty-five and forty-five years of age. Somewhat frizzy, reddish-brown hair, it's going to be about four inches long. From the bite wounds, you don't even want my thoughts on the kind of mouth he's packing. He might have some kind of syndrome or disorder, like gigantism caused by hypersecretion—something that causes bone problems. He's going to be, no less than seven feet tall if there's disproportion to his hands and feet. I suspect there'd have to be because of the size of hands and feet we're talking about. We're talking hands like a sheet of paper and twenty inch feet. If they were proportionate we'd be talking about a guy closer to nine feet tall," he craned his neck away from the pictures and smiled when he added, "but we're not."

"He's going to weigh about four hundred pounds, maybe four-fifty, depending on what the ground was like—hard to say not being there. From your pictures, I'd say it's a reasonable guess. I think your thoughts about this being some separatist or wild man might be spot on. By the time the disorder was in full bloom, I can see a parent giving little thought to abandoning their little freak somewhere—enough parents do that to perfectly healthy children. He might be completely feral. An alternative to that hypothesis might be that this guy grew up in society and fled it because people like to be assholes. He might be pissed off beyond reason. I take it you're not open to asking around about any guy like this, or a child someone knew of that might have been a little 'off' and disappeared?"

"We don't really want this getting all over the place. I think they're content to justify themselves afterward, if the killer is a man… If we asked you to, could you hunt a man?"

Jeffrey considered this without looking like he was considering anything but the lovely evening and trees around his yard.

I couldn't read his tone when he answered, if it was somber, or flat or just saying, "I told you, I hunt everything."

"Are you any good?" I hoped I wasn't being insulting.

"I've put in my time with guns," he returned. "I can do you one better, Patterson. If I can find him, I'll kill him. If he finds me and he's more than I can deal with—all the Vietcong and hundreds of landmines didn't get me—I can promise that no wild man will either."

"I'll hold you to that," I agreed uneasily. He raised an issue I, in my peerless selfishness hadn't considered, how safe this was for the hunter.

"Do you know another good guy to go with you?" I asked.

Green shook his head.

"You hunt with someone else if you want to carry on and don't mind if you succeed or not. This guy killed five people…he pulverized five helpless people. I'll kill him on my own. If I could, I'd fuckin' kill him twice."

"What kind of pay would you want?"

He laid the pictures face down on the manila folder.

"It's on the house."

CHAPTER NINE

I had a feeling Jeffrey Green was just about as happy as I was to have an incident like this fall into the peaceful world we thought we were sold up here. By the time I left, he was looking at the woods differently—although it might have been my imagination. The whole time I was with him I felt an air of perfectly synchronized multitasking in the former soldier. He was aware of me and gave me the appropriate amount of his thoughts while sifting through the information I gave him and also, I believe, being aware of what was going on around us like he was standing in a ranger tower with high-powered binoculars. I had a feeling Jeffrey Green was going to be able to find this man and we could put all of it behind us—soon. Maybe even Doug Napier could too.

Later, when I explained to Chuck how Green ended up agreeing to hunt the bear or bastard, he was relieved—like the worst was halfway over and couldn't wait to tell the others.

By the time I got home, David Schaller already had a fine piece of word-of-mouth going. Part of the success in that was on account of Schaller's notoriety for being tight-lipped—and people were going to run with anything that fell out of it. The first thing out of my wife's mouth was, "They got the bear."

Then she saw my face, I don't know what was on it, but she sat down and asked me what it was.

I told her that I'd heard the interview with Napier and what he said matched up with what I saw at Lot 9 and how the ranger, Paul Ketchum, explained things happened. I told her how Napier said the thing was big and too narrow to be a bear and he was right. I told her what Jeffrey Green said and she blanched. The next time I saw her look like that was when our daughter called to tell us one of our great-grandsons died.

She agreed when I told her what myself, Schaller, Hoffman and Krantz figured, that it was better that people didn't know what we were really dealing with and that tomorrow morning the former school teacher was going to start tracking him down.

She wondered if there'd be any problems with us sending a hunter out into the park and I explained to her that Green was probably off the phone already with Ketchum and that hikers and campers weren't allowed beyond the busy camping areas near the Visitor's Center. If this guy is just in the park, we're talking about seven hundred acres—but if Green is right and he's actually living in the National Forest—Green will have more than a million acres to himself."

"Not completely to himself," Rosie tensely reminded. I could see she was pretty scared, this bad news slammed into the face of good news.

I wasn't about to tell her about the camper up there with all the kids who said she had that thing looking at her all day and lustily, which suddenly occurred to me might not be as far-fetched as I'd first taken it. Everybody needs contact and everybody gets lonely. There was no telling how often this thing stalked ladies in the park. Female hikers encountered him too and were filled with dread—sometimes people know without knowing…and then suddenly I felt like *I* knew. June Napier was a fairly striking woman, with captivating eyes, a cute figure and dazzling golden hair. I had a feeling that thing had been watching June and, like I knew animals do, meant to kill her whelps and savage her. I thought of the broadly smudged and crushed ground where June had fought him. I thought of the heels of her bare feet cutting furrows in the earth. I bet she was fighting for more than just her and her family's lives. I suddenly felt like I knew why he targeted the Napier's and not one of the other nearby camps.

"Pat?" my wife called me out of my reeling thoughts. I looked at her and felt pain at the thought of losing her and anything hurting her. I was ashamed to feel the threat of tears, but successfully overcame them. Concern deepened her ageless eyes and I marveled at the youthful her, under a veneer of obligatory age. There were lines that remembered every expression she ever made and every word she ever said. There were strands of white that added sparkle to her acorn-brown hair and I thought her every age lovely. What happened to June Napier in the early hours of August 3rd, 1983 engraved a deeper appreciation for my wife, I am ashamed to this day that it wasn't present to that degree before it.

Not that a lot of people want to think of people in their sixties making love, but two nights before Jeffrey Green disillusioned us of every comfort reality, as we know it—I took my wife at our kitchen table and the blue linoleum with flecks of gold. Since I was eighteen and never after has sex been like it was that evening.

I'm telling you because I'm still proud of it and I'm not sorry for doing that to you. Maybe be grateful that I haven't invested a lot in descriptions of the people I'm talking about—the intention was for sake of those peoples' anonymity, not your nausea. Be grateful, I could have been exceedingly more descriptive about everything that happened—it might have warranted telling of the things I did that I'd never done before then—had it been my autobiography and not about the incident. Get over it, it's not a big part of the story—I'm going to get over it too so I can move on to what happened next.

*   *   *

I was just nodding off when the phone rang. Luckily I was already in the kitchen, so I got it by the third ring.

"Hello," I slurred into the receiver.

"Sorry it's so late," Green's voice came on the line.

"No problem. Is something wrong?" I was sure he was going to tell me that, for one reason or other, he'd changed his mind or an authority at the park or forest wouldn't permit us to do this.

"I want to get an early start at this before too much sign is lost. Hoffman, Krantz, Schaller, Paul and Hill are all supposed to be at the Deb's Drive-Inn south of the park by five tomorrow morning—not fifteen minutes later or I'll be long gone and you can tell them what I said. Krantz says we need Hill on board because of the Death Records. Paul and Krantz want to discuss some things about where Sheriff's Department meets the powers of National Forest Services."

"But you're going to begin in the park, right?"

I heard, "Mm-hmm."

My heart was starting to pound in my ears, adrenaline rushing through me—I knew this feeling well—I was involved in the story now and wanted to tell it. What was happening was the biggest things to ever happen in Okanogan County or many other counties for that matter. I wanted it kept quiet as much as the rest of them, for the sake of our community. Even though my career was all but over, as far as "real news" goes—it wasn't feeling over and the news was feeling very real. I was thinking about my career and thinking about the freakish wild man, the murders and the "sexy" angle of the lustful lunatic.

"Okay. I'll be there."

CHAPTER TEN

I thought we'd all sit down for a cup of coffee while we talked shop, but I guess I should have known better. I hoped the men wouldn't be too bitchy if I said I really fucking needed some coffee, would they mind waiting one damn second while I got one.

I'm not a morning person.

When I turned in, my lights cut across Ketchum and Green's waists. Hoffman, Schaller and Krantz were just behind them and George Hill was standing there, looking like the kid who wants to play, but nobody has even acknowledged he was there. I didn't feel bad for him. In fact, my only other thought toward him was, *Don't bring up the hair.* Hill's work space wasn't exactly organized, so I didn't expect any problems, but there was a different one.

"Jesus, did somebody die?" was the first thing out of my mouth, then a chuckle—at the time I was pretty amused with the joke, myself, tact not being my strong suit, I guess—I was an asshole a lot.

Other than Hill, still looking "lost puppy" the others looked grim. I sobered up pretty darn quick.

"What the hell's going on?" I wanted to know.

"You guys are going to have to make some decisions here on your own—I assume you'll all tell him what he missed?" Jeffrey Green said.

"What's the rush?" I demanded. I looked at my watch, but couldn't read it in the dark. I wished they'd been standing around in the front where there were lights.

"Go on, tell 'im," Green hurried while fishing his keys out of his jean's pocket. I appreciate, if I was late, that he didn't throw it in my face.

"There might be other murders," Paul Ketchum told me what, by their faces, all the others already knew.

"Say again?"

"I've been on the phone with some people to make sure Jeffrey will be expected out in the park or the National Forest—so people in the departments will stay clear of the areas as much as possible over the next couple days and won't put a bead on him, should they see this armed fella tromping through the woods. I got the 'why he's there' and that all covered—" Ketchum waved Green off when he hurried away from the group, the jingling of keys marked his passage through the darkness on the other side of the lot. "—but I found out some things from him and from the sheriff here that suggest we might have a bigger problem than we thought."

Then it was Krantz's turn.

"After Green called Hoffman and he updated me on what you all figured was going on, I did a little light research on children and adults in the area who might fit the basic description I got. I didn't see anything promising, but I did come across a lot of complaints and reports in a reasonably close area regarding a large man spotted on people's properties, even trying to break into homes. The descriptions vary from pretty damn close, to pretty far out, but we're talking about scared people. To hear Napier go on is proof of what fear will do to a guy's mind."

"Why is that a bigger problem?" I shrugged.

"What it shows us is that this guy might have made a lot of failed attempts at people who were on their home turfs and able to deal with him," Schaller cut in. It was probably way too long since he heard his own voice. "So he's learning that he can be more successful with people who are out on their own, behind thin walls, or strolling through dense woods, who knows how far, between them and anybody."

I looked at Paul for an explanation, but I got it from Chuck.

"There have been some missing persons reports sent up here because people somewhere else thought their friends or family had come up here to camp or hike, even runaways. John and Paul compared notes and we're looking at mostly the same area and the majority of them in the past five weeks. We're talking about missing people. Some of them we knew were registered at the park, but we aren't always informed when people leave. With the National Forest? Who would know? What we *do* know is that this is too much to be a coincidence. We have a real bad guy out there who might have bodies scattered all over this place or he might have prisoners—"

"Or they might be safe and sound, working odd jobs in Oregon or Idaho," Hill grunted. They all looked at him. They all looked annoyed. I had a feeling that I missed some friction in my apparent lateness.

"Yeah, they might," Chuck pacified.

"There's a pattern too," Hill said smartly, dabbing his finger at the middle of the circle of men like adding his thoughts to a pool.

I rolled my eyes, without any reason but not particularly liking Hill that morning—peer pressure?

No one seemed interested in filling me in on that part. I didn't even feel like asking him to explain it to me, assuming the others already knew. I also didn't feel like I would have to ask. I was not to be disappointed.

"These 'abductions', these imaginary 'attacks' and—if there were any real ones—all take place in a time frame that supports my original conclusions!" I realized he was directing this at Paul Ketchum.

"You still think it's a bear?" I guessed.

"It *is* a bear!" Hill snapped, spittle struck my face, neck and hand.

I very, very nearly punched him square in the face. "Why?"

"To say nothing of the extensive report I drew up about the deaths and their causes—if these people are in any way related to this isolated incident we are more or less still talking about a sick bear. Almost all of these reports and inquiries about 'missing' people take place between July and October. We would most definitely be talking about a starving, hungry, parasite infested mongrel who is trying to get ready for hibernation!" he jabbed his finger in my face one time short of when I promised myself I'd break it if he did it again.

"Don't ever put your finger in my face again," David Schaller warned coolly.

Sheriff Krantz's face was saying the same thing.

"It doesn't even matter," Chuck, the peace maker, intervened. "Obviously all, you all, have good reasons for feeling like you do. Now we all know that if there is any mangy, sickly bear out there that Jeffrey isn't going to just ignore it, especially if it's got blood on it. We're not ruling out a bear, but he's going to be looking for a man too."

"Fine, but I'm not changing my report," Hill said defiantly.

"Good, then that keeps our story straight, doesn't it?" Schaller patted the shorter, softer, man on the shoulder.

"If there's some son-of-a-bitch out there, the world is better off, his victims are better off, our community is better off not even knowing he existed," Hoffman mumbled.

"What if there are prisoners?" my journalistic mouth was watering.

"Then we'll have to say we made a mistake, even though we 'did kill and burn a sick bear' who was a likely suspect and we were never expecting this," Krantz explained.

"Agreed," Hoffman nodded. Schaller nodded slowly. Hill was rolling his eyes. I know he did because he rolled his head too.

"Let's take a break, please, get some coffee," I moaned. "I barely have a head on today."

"Yeah, I could use something too," Schaller rubbed his eyes. I thought he looked pretty shabby.

As we were walking around to the front of the diner, George Hill caught me by the elbow and turned me.

Three strikes, I thought, *next time you bother me you're out.*

"Where did you put the hairs?" he sounded so accusing that he got a rise of new anger in me.

"On your desk," I sounded bewildered, or at least I tried to.

"Charlie Hoffman came over to compare notes and they weren't there to show him. He wanted a sample to send to Seattle!"

"What do you want me to do about it?"

"Well, you were the last person to touch them."

"Was I?" I launched a full blown angry elder tone. Clearly I had been too respectful to this guy already because he sure thought he could talk to me like I was a piece of shit now.

I expected the little shithead to back down a little bit and he did, just a little, but he was clearly very angry and my gut told me it had very little to do with the hairs.

"Don't take it out on me if those guys don't think it's a bear anymore," I guessed. "I'm just here because I saw some questionable things so I asked questions—that's kind of what I do…"

"And what I do is look at injuries or organs or whatever I have to, to know what happened to a person that made them need my services. I think I know a little more about this than *any* of you!"

"Let me guess," I raised my eyebrows and cocked my head to the right. "You told *them* that too?"

Hill raised his finger to argue something else and I slapped his soft and clammy hand away.

"I need some fucking coffee, Hill, and then, if you still want some hair I'll pull it out of my head, because it's the only hair I have!"

I stomped angrily into the warm light and blinking red "OPEN" sign, where the others already since passed.

I was pleased with myself and felt rewarded by the aroma of fresh coffee and all kinds of delicious breakfast foods that would probably be considered too fatty and too large a serving by today's standards. That's why so much food costs too much for what you get and tastes like shit, if you're lucky, because it's more flavor than you'd get otherwise.

Deputy Schaller wanted to know how I'd found a hunter so fast and if I thought he would be any good. So I told him why I met Green and shrugged about the rest.

"I wouldn't know Robin Hood from Dick Grayson."

"Maybe one of us should have just went or several of us," Schaller was shaking his head and looking very, very tired under the too white suspended lighting. "This is a police matter."

"Police use civilians all the time," I said offhandedly—my coffee was being poured.

"Well, one of us could have gone with," he returned.

"There are few enough of us as it is," Krantz objected. "We don't have the manpower to send one of ours out hunting."

"Hunting a murderer? Isn't that our job?" Schaller put bluntly. "I can't say for you, John, but calls aren't exactly eating up my free time."

"Well," the sheriff blustered, "what stopped you then? You local boys want to piss away your time on what any able, sound-minded guy with a semi-decent weapon can do? What would stop you? Me, I just have the whole *county* to—"

"Don't be a jackass—"

"—a what?!"

"You heard me, jackass," Schaller and Krantz were both out of their seats and yelling at each other across the table. Their fingers were in each other's faces and, I hate it so much for myself that I was annoyed, at the moment, just seeing it.

"*You* listen—" Krantz began.

"NO! You fucking *listen*!" Schaller thundered, his finger finally making contact with the man it was angry at and didn't exactly poke him lightly. "Suppose this guy hauls off and shoots somebody out there—just *somebody*— then how do we explain to the public how we sent this guy, we don't really know, out there to kill someone or something we know has *slaughtered* at least five people!"

Sheriff Krantz's face looked like it was going to pop. It was well past red and into shades of purple then.

"Don't you ever—" Krantz trembled with rage.

"Just shut your damn face," Deputy Schaller spat. "Put your goddamn 'look at my badge, everybody better kiss my ass' ego away and think about what I just said to you. Jesus H. Christ. Wou—"

"I can vouch for him, if that's what you need," Paul Ketchum offered. He seemed unfazed by the angry transaction. Since he dealt with the public in a more social way, I assume he was accustomed to keeping his cool. Then he lowered his voice, "But we can't be discussing it like this in public."

"It would be your neck too," Hoffman warned Ketchum.

"I can live with that."

"If he fucks up like that, we cut him loose and none of this ever happened," Krantz told us, not asked us.

I saw the ranger's eyes reject the glare that twitched on them momentarily. Hoffman looked stunned. Schaller and Krantz looked stonily at each other.

That was when George Hill won a few more hearts:

"I don't know about the rest of you, but I apparently have more to do than even you, Sheriff—*I* need to get back to my office."

"I'll go talk to Debbie," Hoffman offered, if Ketchum would let him out of the seat.

While he was standing up, Paul took the opportunity to spot all the witnesses to the exchange. There was a cook in the back, now standing at the sending/receiving window between him and Debbie, at the counter. A trucker, working on his breakfast, would go home to Utah or Nebraska, or wherever, with stories of the bizarre locals in Okanogan—don't you doubt it.

Beside me, John Krantz was saying he better "git" and I got up to let him through. His unlikely broad hip, considering his legs were so small, jarred the table and three of our cups spilled over into the saucers below them. I almost called him a jackass too.

Schaller put his cup back down, it rattled tellingly before finding the right spot to trust.

"What's on your mind?" I asked.

"What do you think's on my mind," he replied.

"Jeff Green?" I supposed.

"Barely," he was picking on the plastic trim around the tabletop. "Think more along the lines of a dead family and a killer that's still running free and at least you'd be in the same universe."

I apologized. He shook his head and said it didn't matter, that there was a lot on his mind.

"I just want the safety of the citizens that count on me," I barely heard him say as he shifted to the end of the pumpkin orange vinyl booth. "All this happened in my town, not yours or the next one over. What else could I be thinking about?"

I apologized again, but he didn't hear or ignored me. He tossed his hand in a goodbye wave to Hoffman and then he was gone too.

I was thinking that all these guys realized how big it was a lot sooner than I did. I wasn't liking myself that much, just then. Not very much at all.

By the end of the week, I remember feeling certain I would go to hell when I die.

CHAPTER ELEVEN

That day in August, even for August, felt particularly humid. I remember because I felt like I was damp all the time and I remember that because I didn't really do much but sit around feeling uncomfortable, waiting for news. Occasionally a merciful gust would push across our deck and lend the least amount of relief. I wondered what it was like in the woods and how far Green had travelled. Mostly I was wondering if he found anything or if he was just hoping to pick up a trail.

The few of us who knew about the critical hunt going on that day, we were like a secret society, I felt.

It was otherwise a gorgeous Sunday mid-morning and the grandkids were playing down in the yard while the wife and daughter sat in dark green plastic lawn chairs and carried on about this or that. There I was, perched above them, grimly aware of something happening that most of the world was oblivious too…and would remain oblivious to, until now.

It wasn't a good feeling. I didn't feel special. I felt privileged, but not special. If there's no difference to you, fair enough, but they were strongly distinguishable attributes to me that day.

Yesterday, probably, Doug Napier got a visit from the preacher and plans were likely made for putting his family to their final rest. It was many years later, when talking to Chuck, that I found out that part of the reason Hill was being such a dick that morning was because Napier didn't want him to do the services and hadn't heard it until Chuck told him. I guess that Hill was pushing and pushing Chuck for the best time to make the arrangements and finally he just had to tell Hill that Napier had other plans. George would get his pound of flesh for that offense.

I also heard that Napier got the word about the sick bear being killed and that he still denied it was a bear. So that was getting around too. I don't know if that would help or hurt us, but I wished that the officers involved in this conspiracy had thought to put some kind of "hush" order on the nursing staff—where, to this day, I'm sure is where the word first got out. All of that raised the issue that we didn't have a lot of time before one story would outgrow the other and if the "Sasquatch" story got too big, everything we were afraid would happen surely would.

I wrote up an article this morning that said the alleged bear remains were tested and were positive for several parasites and, in the shadow of *Cujo,* rabies. I considered saying that human remains were found when the stomach was opened, but I didn't dare—not if Jeff Green found captives with the creeper.

If *that* turned out to be the case, I didn't know what we could do to stop getting a lot of publicity for it, but I knew if I smelled the big wigs in media smelling the story, I was going to have a damn good article ready to hit the presses before they got to ask where it happened. I'd have the article sold by the time they actually found it. I'd get undeserved acclaim for articles and recognition where, in Spokane, I was competing with a lot of excellent writers and was visible only every now and then, like a drowning man. I was thinking, if any reporter was going to profit from this, it was going to be me.

Ultimately, no one was going to profit from it and the losses would come dear.

*   *   *

I couldn't tell you how many times I was asked, that day, if I was alright. But I do think that the only answer I gave was, "Yeah. Yeah."

Maybe someone should have gone with him, I remember thinking more than once.

I thought about Napier and the shape he was in after dealing with the guy.

I wondered if Green was spending the night out in the woods.

It was getting late. I'd counted almost every minute pass wondering if it would be the next one or the next.

Is someone being killed right now?

Grandpa was no fun at all, but I didn't particularly find the grandkids much fun either, they were getting past the cute stage and I didn't understand their taste in music and I didn't like their hair.

Hoffman called once to see if I wanted to come over for a drink after his shift. He called later to see if I'd changed my mind.

I looked down at the notes I was taking, now blurring in the fading sunlight, and felt for the first time in recollection, overwhelmed with information...and I didn't really know anything yet.

*   *   *

The phone rang at around nine Monday morning. I'd been up since before the pants slid down the butt crack of dawn and everything outside was very dark and, I felt, menacing. I was jumping at every sound and wondering what it was, even though I knew what it was—it wouldn't register fast enough to do me any good.

A lot of things in nature make sounds you can't imagine them making in the day—a rabbit's cry, the strange human-like call of a fox that seems to ask "How?" "How?", a bob cat's scream and giant grey owls that don't hoot, but bark like disembodied dogs. I have, in my time, heard sounds that I never made any sense of and I know I am in good company of city slickers out in the sticks wetting their britches over something any woodsman would dismiss. There are some sounds that even experienced outdoorsman have never been able to attach to anything they know, no matter how often they've heard it, no matter who they ask, no matter what calls they compare it to. After that night there would be one sound locals would report no longer hearing. There would be no more reports of strange men or otherwise being spotted on the roadways, in the park, in people's yards. No one would go through the horror of having that person, or otherwise, rattling at their locked door, staring in through their window, threatening them on hiking trails or killing their livestock.

On the other end of the line someone said:

"He got it."

I wanted to know where he was—how he was, but the undiscernible male caller just said that it was all he knew.

Now I know that anybody else who got that call was going to do what I was about to and that was haul ass out to Jeffrey Green's. I figured, unless that was Chuck, I would be the last person to get the word. I was, after all, the person who had the least right to be involved.

I kissed the side of my wife's head while I pulled on my heavy tan cardigan. I told her I had to leave and not to wait for me at lunch.

I drove too fast and, in the back of my mind, kept thinking that the only three police in a hundred miles were at Jeff Green's house. This was an exaggeration, but it didn't feel like much of one.

I didn't take speeding as seriously as I did decades later. You have to remember—well, maybe you don't—that seatbelt use wasn't even mandatory in Britain until 1983—a completely different age and consciousness. My wife was told to drink when she was nursing our daughter and it would help the baby rest. People could still smoke in hospitals. Anyway, you get the difference. At least parts.

I wasn't at all surprised to see the patrol cars, two city and one county and the little green foreign car I remembered seeing at Hill's. Neither did it surprise me that, like when I called on him two days ago, Green hadn't invited them inside.

Chuck waved at me and I waved back.

Nervous might not be the best word for how I felt walking up to that group of men, but it's what I got. The first face I looked for was Jeffrey Green's. He looked agitated and a little frightened, but the muscles in his face were too tense to emote feelings.

"You got him?" I raised the most cheerful inflection into my question.

Jeffrey Green nodded and then he started to shake.

"It's okay," Chuck hurried.

Schaller caught me by my left shoulder and turned me out into the yard.

"We were just getting him calm," the deputy scolded. Then said to himself, "I can just hear Duncan telling me this was just how Napier was."

"What?" I demanded.

"He's scared, but he says he killed it. He said he found skeletons so he knew—"

"It?"

Schaller looked me in the eyes and the severity in his seriousness awoke a childlike fear in me—like a parent leaning in to bark the order to run to the storm shelter.

I looked at the other men and realized that Green was the only one sitting and that struck me as something he wouldn't otherwise do if there were guests standing around him. My mind wanted to dwell on this, I think, because it was more comfortable than the conversation I was about to have.

"That's what he's been saying," David Schaller said at last. "My guess was that he was chased or had fallen for another reason. His clothes were dirty in all the right places. He's washed his face and hands, but the undersides of his wrists are streaked with dirt and white lines where pebbles and crap made little furrows in the first couple layers of skin."

"Did he end up fighting out there?" I worried.

"It looks like it, but he's not saying much. Mostly he just wanted to let us know it was dead. He called Paul first and after he did a little tending to his pal, called the rest of us."

I told him I wanted to see Green and he warned me about getting him upset. I wouldn't know how to prevent or provoke that and sensitivity was not my strongest attribute.

"Was it a bear?" I asked Green.

"Sure," he said quickly.

"If you're not going to cooperate—" Krantz was even less sensitive than me.

"What difference does it make if what's responsible is dead?" Ketchum fired back.

"I need to know exactly what's going on," Krantz was dead serious. "Now, if there's a man laying up there shot then you need to say so Jeff, so it can be taken care of. This thing is going to blow wide open if someone stumbles across this—"

"I don't think they will," Green mumbled.

"I don't care what you think, I need guarantees. Now I know you didn't drag any body or any thing out of that forest, right?"

"Obviously," Green snapped.

"So we have a problem. You're going to need to go back and either bring us the man or we'll just let the bear story hold. But I need the facts, mister. I need them now."

"How can I tell you the facts? All I can do is tell you what I found."

I spotted a few strands of reddish brown hair in the folds of the elbow of his jacket when he unfolded his arms and braced his hands on his knees. I don't think it was missed on George Hill either, since he was barely blinking, waiting to be vindicated on his cause of death report.

Green asked Ketchum to get him a beer. After two and a glass of water he resigned himself to tell us.

"I got on the trail at Lot 9 and followed it out of the park, crossed Twenty, the river there and into the national forest. I could see where the general area had been passed now and then before, in regular use, but not using one fauna freeway like deer and things do where sometimes the grass doesn't even grow anymore. I was concerned about messing one trail up for another, but the drips of blood helped."

"I felt pretty confident about catching up or finding the guy—the further I went, the stronger that smell got."

"I followed the tracks for some time and reached a steep rise over one of those streams, like fly-fishing heaven, that flood so bad in the spring and run low the rest of the year. The smell was stronger than ever there. The slope was incredibly steep, but the path veered down there and I wasn't there to not follow it. Before I got a chance to make up my mind the best way to handle it, I heard a dull thumping sound to the southwest…

Jeffrey looked in the direction of the sound. Directly parallel to him, in the dim light of the dense covered woods he saw a bear with its front paws planted firmly on the trunk of a fallen tree. The sickly looking creature seemed very thin and long because of its thinness. In the shadows, its face looked disfigured, like someone shot off most of its mug. His mind reeled against the facts I'd laid out and he was thinking, it must be half-starved. No wonder it wasn't biting. No wonder it was so aggressive. One shit shot during hunting season and the bear, plump for hibernation, though suffering, survives the winter, but the next year is another thing. It starts to become brazen because the alternative is death. Who knows what all it'd been through? Jeffrey Green knew all too well about what trauma can do to a living thing. The madness or shyness abuse causes in animals. If lunacy is a possible side effect of suffering in humans, then it can surely be in animals too. It can—

It was looking right at him.

Jeffrey raised his rifle and steadied it on the dull space between the shine of its shaded eyes.

Then it raised up its paws and drove them up and down against the trunk—that's when Green noticed it had a rock in its hands.

Hands?

Darkness filled the lens. The scope dropped away from his eye and the thing was charging him and howling and beating its fists on anything as it went by.

Without thinking one way or another, Jeffrey ran and tripped and rolled over and over himself until colliding with a tree trunk. The thing tumbled after him, no matter what it looked like, it was controlled. It would redirect itself by catching a tree and would unfold its legs just enough to slow it.

Green didn't feel that he had any other choice but to keep going down. There was no way to outrun it moving uphill, and while he was light on his feet, it was too dangerous to run parallel to the steep hill where tripping again was almost guaranteed. This looked manageable. Down the river it might look like death.

When the slope got so steep that Jeffrey had to turn on his belly and climb down, the thing—right above him—made a sound that made his heart pound so hard with fear that hours later he could still feel it ringing in his ears. It was something like a howl or a wail. It had a strange vocalization to it that would stay in Green's mind for the rest of his days—it would be the last waking memory of countless nightmares.

There were no more than three heavy footsteps and then it landed on the ground to the right of him, below.

Conscious of exactly where his gun was, where his hands were, where the thing was—conscious that it barely faltered on its landing and was straightening to its full, horrifying height, conscious that it could surely climb faster than he could—Jeffrey let go of the embankment.

It charged.

Green hit the rocky shore on his left leg and buttock and the hand that kept him from falling completely.

The gunshot rang through the tall steep walls of the river bottom, raising birds and driving deer to hoof.

Then Green himself made a sound, somewhere between a scream and a sigh, and slumped backward onto the melon-sized rocks and let this terrible sound until he couldn't anymore. Relief and surprise bred the sound he never made before or after that day. He'd heard a similar sound come out of other people—like when a lover or parent is reunited with someone they thought was lost forever.

The sprawled mass of tangled fur lay out on the rocks a mere yard and a half away. Just laying his eyes on it brought tremors and tears so it was some time before he was able to get himself together, or even stand.

He studied the thing, but wouldn't touch it, not even with one of the long pieces of driftwood scattered here or there on the shore.

Twice more he shot it in the head, because, he said, he couldn't have turned his back on it otherwise. When finally he did turn his back he found himself staring into a suspicious washout in the embankment—one that stunk.

Taking a moment to recheck his supplies, especially for anything that could have been lost or broken in the fall, Jeffrey faced down the black mouth under the bank, constantly aware of his gun.

It was getting late then and Jeffrey knew he wouldn't be close to getting out of the woods before nightfall. So he put on his headlamp and stooped enough to walk into the pitch black space.

If there were any others they would either be in there or out here, he reasoned. If they were inside, he'd kill them as he found them. If they were coming home, he'd kill them as they found him.

"It went on for some ways," Jeffrey told us. "It wasn't but eight feet into it when it was obviously dug out. After about fifty feet it opened up into the den. There weren't any other passages, as far as I could tell. Up until then, it would have had to go in almost completely hunched, but in the large room it would have only had to stoop because I could stand there. The earth was packed and had been for ages, it was almost like rock, except for the strange short mounds of earth in the center of the room. They were clearly old, but hadn't been walked on like the rest of the earth. There was a huge stone in there. It was a river rock, almost flat on the top side and pretty close on the bottom. It looked like other flat rocks had been wedged in underneath it. It was pretty level."

Hill muttered something then, but I wasn't listening and Green didn't stop talking—at that point I don't know if he could or if he did what it would take to get going again.

"Behind it, on a higher table of packed earth there was a corpse that must have been laying there for a year or however long to get it to that state of decomposition. It was just covered in rotting mush. It was in front of it, and all around it really, that I found pieces of, what looked like, human skeletons. There might have been animal bones too, but they were mostly smashed to nothing. There was a pretty big rock on the flat stone and it had seen a lot of use over a lot of time. It was smooth and crudely shaped, like a primitive pestle."

"On the other side of the room I found a corner with a lot of droppings. They had a lot of nuts and seeds in them and fish scales. There was a pretty expansive part covered in bedding—field grass and cedar branches—but it didn't look like but one part of it was being used. It's "nest" was deeper and fresher."

"So was it a bear?" Chuck asked. "Did you check its mug?"

"It chased me on two legs," Green reminded stiffly.

"Bear are capable of that," Hill pointed.

"The hell they can," Ketchum objected.

"I've seen them walk on their hind legs!" Hill demurred.

"Thank you! Yes, *walk*—just like a toddler," the ranger agreed.

"Did you take a look at it?" it was Krantz's turn to ask.

"I wasn't sure, but when I got back I consulted some texts. I think it might have been a meganthropus or homo Heidelbergensis," he didn't wait to hear that we didn't know what that was, because he hadn't even heard of it before that morning himself. "No remains of either have been found in the America's, but if you want a rational answer, that's all I have for you. It's not a giant. Napier's right, that was no bear either."

"But those have got to be ancient species," I reasoned.

"That's right, they are, so it couldn't be exactly what it was 250,000 years ago, but we're not either."

"So why would it be here? Why wouldn't there be remains all over? Like that Bigfoot—wouldn't someone find a body somewhere?"

Schaller agreed.

"Maybe not," Jeffrey offered tentatively. "Homo Heidelbergenesis' brain was almost the same size as people's. They might think the same way as we do, at least about certain things."

"What are you getting at?" Hill blurted.

"I think they bury each other," the hunter suggested. "I think any number of those bones at that flat stone were of its kind. I think they crush them, like we cremate ours. I think that skeleton rotting behind it was one of them, working itself out until the time that they bury them. I noticed two things right there, that skeleton was big and the ground around, what I make to be like an altar, was white and crunchy with bone. All bone."

Paul Ketchum was about to speak, but Green went on without noticing, "There are how many hundreds and thousands of river miles where you would never see one of these holes. Hundreds and thousands of unpredictable river miles that do hellable, destructive things to whatever is in their path. I think you don't see them and people are only going to see less because they're dying out. There aren't enough to populate. That means one generation and 'poof' that's it, for a loner like I think this was. I think they have burial practices like primitive man has always had. I think there was something wrong with this thing, I think it was old, hungry and lonely and one hundred percent mental because of it. It was old. I could see it the way you see age in a dog—it was real old."

We all sat quietly for the longest time. It had been a few days since June Napier's brother told me a Sasquatch had attacked the family. It was all but out of my mind and wouldn't register, no matter how sure Green was. How do you accept the unacceptable? I don't think you can, not unless you see it with your own eyes or science proves it to you. Science wasn't going to get a chance to prove this to us, not then, not thirty years later. I would never see it with my own eyes, but my mind conjured something to match the strange footprint we found. A footprint that, only then, did I let myself think could be anything other than human.

The sheriff was the first to break the stunned silence—he'd either come up with his ultimate conclusion pretty quick or had a back-up plan all along, "Do you think you can find that place again?"

"Yes," Green said surely.

"You need to go back up there and destroy the bodies. You need to cave in the mouth of the den."

I remember that we all looked toward Krantz like we were in a drunken daze. It was then that I first realized that Chuck had slid into a seat.

A look of realization crossed David Schaller's face first and then he nodded repeatedly to himself.

"There were no complete human skeletons?" Krantz pressed.

"No. I just suspected some of the bones were human."

"That's fine," John Krantz affirmed. "But the whole point of this is that nothing too big for this community falls on it."

"So what next?" Schaller said steadily.

"You know your part, Jeff," the sheriff nodded to him. "But we need to clean up some loose ends here and fast."

"What kind of loose ends?" Chuck Hoffman asked.

"First of all, Hill, you are going to need to amend your reports. All these files, the tapes and transcripts and maybe some of the police photos will have to be destroyed. We can't have any leaks. Agreed?"

Hill was aghast, but the rest of us at least agreed that out small community not be torn inside out by the media.

"Patterson, I'm really going to need you to not do a big sensational story about this—it just needs to go away. We're not just talking about Bigfoot nut-balls up here, we're talking about news and scientists—turning our community inside out for one dead thing—one violent murdering thing."

I agreed not to write about it.

"You know if word gets out about this none of you is going to get any peace—not one of you," Krantz seemed to say to Green and Ketchum. "Do you want that? Interviews and strangers knocking at your door? Phone calls at all hours? Reporters chasing you?"

Green shook his head. Ketchum appeared to just be listening to the building horror between us.

"If what you say is true, Green, then there's something laying out there dead that thousands upon thousands of people are going to go crazy to get at. You need to make it disappear. That's your fucking mess, clean it up like it never was or God help me you'll be a sorry son-of-a-bitch if I hear someone say they found a body of Bigfoot laying out in those woods."

"I'm already sorry," Green returned in tired anger.

"Everybody from Connolly to Mariott is itching to hear from Doug's own mouth what attacked him and killed his family. A lot of people are going to discount what he says because he's a piece of shit, but a lot of people are going to forget that in their childish, stupid, small town enthusiasm to be a part of the drama themselves. If Doug is adamant enough, other people might be interested in hearing and telling his story and all of this running around will have been for nothing."

"People are going to believe what they want to believe," Schaller said to himself. "Maybe the damage is already done. There are a hundred and one rumors about what happened…"

"Why not just call it what it was?" Hill exclaimed.

"Goddammit!" Krantz raged, red-faced and veins popping. "We got lumber and we got mining and more and better camping than any other county in Washington or maybe any other state, for that matter. What the fuck do you think is going to happen to those summer dollars if people hear that when bear get sick up here they massacre people? People are locking their children and pets inside and between us and forestry the official word is a bear attack, because it was better than a Bigfoot story flocking all kinds of crazies across Okanogan. This bear story is going to keep people away."

"I know some people who own or work at motels and resorts that would go under if that happened," Chuck frowned thoughtfully.

He and the misses lived modestly with her added income and, I figured, his mind went first to the diner where she worked—that mostly catered to out-of-towners. Of course there were bait shops, boat rentals, gift shops, guides and even mechanic shops who counted on the "fun money" and necessary expenses of vacationers.

"What do you suggest?" Deputy Schaller pulled his worried eyes off the decking and fixed them on the sheriff.

"We need to make sure there's no doubt in people's minds about what happened to that poor family. If we leave the blame on the bear, people are going to be asking themselves if we got the right one. The other problem is Napier going around telling people that it wasn't a bear anyway. Nobody would believe him if he said it was dry in the desert, but people always pay attention to gossip and weirdness. We need to fix Napier up in a way where no one will believe him."

The following chapter is based on transcripts taken of the second interview with Doug Napier, tape recorded 8:31am Tuesday,, August 9th, 1983. The questioning was conducted by County Sheriff John Krantz and Palmer Deputy David Schaller. Mariott Deputy Charlie Hoffman listened and served as witness from another room.

Some of the liberties taken with Doug Napier's thoughts and feelings were based on conversations I later had with friends and family regarding the character and history of the Napier family.

CHAPTER TWELVE

"You told us last time that you hadn't used drugs since you got back from Vietnam. You might not know this, but some of them drugs never leave your system—who's to say you weren't tripping on it that night."

"I wasn't."

"You'd just got back from war, Douglas, you don't think you might have sparked up trying to deal with all that?"

"That's not what I did and I gave up the drink."

"When, huh? When'd you give it up?"

"Almost three years ago, alright? And I've only had a few drinks since and none of them in the last year."

"But you do have a drinking problem."

"It hasn't been a problem."

"But you are saying that you turned to the bottle to cope—you were coping with a problem. Is that problem gone or are you still coping? And if you're not drinking what are you coping with? Or are you not coping? Are you not coping at all? I think you cope by taking it out on other people. Look at this—" Schaller slammed a thick file to the table, purging any number of papers from it. "How many times have you been arrested for drunk and disorderly?"

"I—"

"How many times have you been arrested for assault and battery?"

"It—"

"How many times have you been caught drunk driving, driving with no license, breaking and entering—"

"I was just a kid then—"

"—yeah, yeah," Krantz dismissed with a flip of his hand. "How many times did you hit your wife?"

"Too many."

"How many?"

"Too fucking many!" Napier screamed, almost nose to nose with sheriff Krantz.

"How many times did you hit your wife?"

Napier settled back in his chair, dropped his face in his hands and began to sob.

"Are you a violent man, Douglas?"

"I have been."

"How many times did you hit your wife?"

"I don't know. When I was drinking, I don't know, but I knew I dunnit. I was the only one who could have."

"Do you forget what's happened when you get

drunk?"

"That was kinda the point."

"Are you a violent drunk?"

"It seems so."

"And were you drunk the night of August the 2nd?"

"No."

"You didn't have a single drink of booze?"

"No."

"Didn't sneak some along? Did you share one with anybody in another camp?"

"*No.*"

"Well that's funny because you're blood alcohol level was well over the limit."

Napier's eyes widened and he looked stricken between Schaller and Krantz.

"There's no way," he protested.

"Yes there is," Schaller gently insisted.

"But I didn't!"

"Would you even remember?" Krantz laid out slowly and punctuated the sentence with a chuckle.

"The coroner has confirmed that it is your hand prints on the body, your bloody handprints on the log you used to beat your kids to death. We got your skin under your wife's nails—"

"N-No. I didn—and she *never* scratched me—not in all the life I've known her has she even pinched anyone—if she clawed something it was that thing—"

"—and you were drunk out of your mind, Douglas. Drunk out of your war riddled mind."

"No. No! NO! NO! NO! I didn't—no fucking way. I wasn't drunk! I wasn't DRUNK!"

"I'm afraid we have to put you under arrest, Doug," Schaller apologized, and I think with utter sincerity, as he slowly pushed up out of his chair.

He said he saw clouds of doubt start to gather first in Napier's eyes and then his face the longer Krantz laid out the facts for him. Doug Napier knew he was a piece of shit and maybe that meant, to him, he could have done it, even if that's not how he remembered it—he hadn't remembered drinking. How? When? *Why? Why* would he have fell in the bottle again? Since James was born their marriage had seen its best years, maybe even since before the war. They were out there to spend time with each other and hadn't said more than a few hellos to their neighbors in the other campgrounds—except the other kids that theirs played with—so he didn't know how he could have got any, even if he wanted some and he didn't, not even now. When could he have done it? June was helping him stay sober. He was barely ever out of her sight and he didn't drink in front of the kids—he *never* drank in front of them. There was no reason why he would have fell off the wagon, but the confusion in this moment felt familiar and that only made it worse and more believable, except that it wasn't believable to Napier—

"I could never do that..."

The cuffs made the rapid metallic clinking of a toy machine gun as they adjusted to the weeping man's wrists.

"Anything you say can and will be held against you..."

"I couldn't..."

The interview room door opened and I heard the solid, awkward first steps of the Tin Man of Oz in those taken by Doug Napier as he left that little room. I can imagine how desperate he must have looked, but Schaller later told me Doug had a look on his face like he was turning inside out to make sense of it—the kind of confusion reserved from the worst kind of trauma or the severest and cruelest aging.

EPILOGUE

O n their own accord the police officers involved destroyed or altered their records. One afternoon John Krantz came to my house and asked me to bring out whatever I had collected over the course of the investigation. This was the first time since childhood that I could remember feeling duress or threatened. A lot of the cops in the area didn't carry guns, but kept them in their patrol units. On no other occasion before had Krantz carried a weapon in my presence—it seemed to really stand out that afternoon when I surrendered my files.

I quietly waited and hoped for someone to come to their senses. Among the good men involved, I thought one of them would do something, but I would never know how hard the other civilians were being leaned on. Chuck Hoffman mentioned to me offhandedly, during the trial, that I had no idea how hard it was to be responsible for so many people.

No, I don't know.

We would never know if those catastrophic events we feared would destroy our homes would come to pass. The reasoning must have amounted to better safe than sorry, but I had a hard time balancing my fears for the future around what we were doing to prevent only possible things from happening. I might be singing a different tune if we'd decided on another solution and either one of those things had happened to our humble little communities and many more lives were ruined. Maybe the reasoning amounted to: the end justifies the means.

Does it?

When?

Just before the trial was set to start I retired from the Palmer newspaper, because it was obvious to me who would be asked to cover the trial. Krantz wanted me to, too. He wanted me to blacken Napier to the public—as if he was actually worried Napier would be acquitted—not with the public defender on Krantz's payroll.

Hoffman and I rarely spoke after that. I suppose some of that was because I wasn't on any local stories and didn't need to tap my resources. The articles I wrote were sold to outside papers and magazines. I couldn't stop writing, but my taste for it had soured. I don't think I'll have any trouble putting down the pen now. I'm sure.

Chuck ran for sheriff and lost to some new hotshot. After the election he opted out of service entirely and started working at the same restaurant as his wife, which would close shop in the economic crash of 2008.

Paul Ketchum picked up and left Washington. I didn't see or hear anything of him for about twenty years.

In the few years after the trial, the word around town was that David Schaller was suffering from alcoholism and had mandatory retirement in 1988.

George Hill's business grew into a chain of three funeral homes, while continuing to do coroner duties at the original locale. I didn't speak to him again nor did any of the others, that I knew of. We all told ourselves we were doing the right thing. I think George Hill told himself, "That's what he gets for doing business somewhere else."

My understanding is that there were no significant changes to Jeff Green's life or livelihood. I think "business as usual" was a lot more effort than he was making it appear, but it was an adjustment he'd gone through before. Green didn't shrink away from society or develop addiction problems, only a heavy silence came over him—his eyes always looked so busy, but not with what lay before him, but to make sense of a memory.

I know that he went back out there and did what he was told. I can't imagine what that was like for him. Ketchum asked about going along with him when the time came to destroy whatever he'd found up there. Green refused. Maybe there was a part of him that was suspicious Ketchum was trying to sabotage the cover up and planned to take pictures of the bodies and cave. More likely, he just didn't want any harm, physical or psychological, to happen to the ranger.

I was with Ketchum while he waited for Green to return. Somehow, impossibly, Jeffrey looked worse. He was filthy and completely exhausted. He barely blinked, sitting in his chair, sipping the beer Paul fetched him while we made small talk around the issue of his state.

It was dark by the time we found out what happened.

He said he was so scared before, entering and leaving the forest, that he completely overlooked that there were all kinds of mounds near the washout that might easily be dismissed as ant hills overgrown with grass and moss. He spent a better part of the day destroying as many as he could, even though he only found what appeared to be bone fragments in two of them.

I could tell, at that point, Green was thoroughly intimidated by the consequences of anything getting out because he missed something. I know he cleaned the scene of evidence like a world class hitman.

Since I've burdened myself with the truth for all these years and even concern for my immortal soul hasn't been enough to break my silence, I don't mind telling you that I have often wished I'd have gotten a chance to see the room for myself. I even looked once. I just wanted to see the damn thing for myself—to get a glimpse at what I thought was impossible—something ethereal and horrible with a face that didn't belong to a drawing or a man in a gorilla costume. I thought I found a place that might have been a demolished mound. That's when I told myself Green wouldn't have left any evidence and ran. I ran like I was running for my life—which probably looked pretty stupid considering I hadn't run for any reason since 1939.

I've always assumed whatever it was, was extinct after that. When I see or hear of people looking for it—for their sake, I hope it is.

I feel like by now you have a pretty good idea about what kind of men were involved in this and are probably wondering how we could have went along with it. That's something I've wondered too.

I often think about Napier's interview and how old lady Whitton came calling on him for church—it was like there was a whole different reality I wasn't privy to—one where not everyone thought Napier was no good. I always knew he was because of the stories I was told—by his own admission he was a piece of shit—but the simplicity of his nature was quickly unravelling and I was faced with someone who would have been easier not knowing.

It wasn't easy for the people who knew Doug—Douglas to his friends. There was a lot of ridicule and some abuse—especially for those who stood by him and a lot of his original supporters did or do to this day, if they are still living.

The Dyers told me they were skeptical that he was really turning his life around, after years of begging June to leave him, but apparently he really was. Contrary to what I was told, a lot of the things I heard weren't true. He did have an extensive record—especially considering there was very little to get up to in Mariott or Palmer or anywhere in Okanogan for that matter. But he hadn't had but a few traffic violations since 1979, the year June was pregnant with James.

On July 8, 2002 Doug Napier, fifty-eight, was finally reunited with his family at their plot at Palmer cemetery after dying of pneumonia at the Washington corrections center near Shelton, where he'd been sentenced to life without parole.

Charlie Hoffman, David Schaller, Jeffrey Green and I attended. George Hill and John Krantz were at other graveyards and had been for some years—it might be judgmental, but I don't think they would have come anyway.

Some of June and Doug's relatives remembered me from the few years after Doug was sentenced, when I made the time to go out and see them. It got too hard after not too long, but I kept visiting until it became unbearable. They thought I'd moved away or passed away. At least they hadn't been thinking badly of me all that this time.

June's sister, April, who even middle-aged bore a striking resemblance to her late sibling, took a good natured jab at Rose-Marie and me, asking how such an old man could still be on his first wife. I know we're lucky to have had as much time as we did and lots of people said so. So to explain our good fortune we always said that neither one of us wanted to leave the other one alone—so in our stubbornness we just didn't.

Rose-Marie did leave, a few years ago now. On her way out she told me she was just going to check it out for us and she'd be back if it wasn't all it was cracked up to be.

When I lost my wife, it made me understand a lot about Doug Napier. I have struggled with my sense of self-worth and morality since then. I haven't felt like a good person or worthy, very often, of the love or kind thoughts or gestures my wife had for me. I don't know what he went through to make him how he was and how much war might have magnified those problems, but I know Napier probably doubted if he deserved June's love. Little else I've known in life has hurt so much as wondering that. When she left, wondering if I could even be with her in Heaven...

Another thing I understand better about Napier is the loss he went through. The mess in the Middle East claimed one of my great-grandsons and disabled another. They were my flesh and blood, true, but they were not my children and it hurt plenty—it hurt awful.

Obviously I'm no spring chicken, so you know my wife wasn't either. Though reasonably healthy, we both accepted the idea that something could happen and maybe quite suddenly. Rose-Marie hung on for days after the heart attacks, until a massive one left mere minutes to say goodbye. It was as if God said, "Enough now, I mean it. It's your time whether you like it or not."

We had already been thinking about the possibility, had plenty of time to feel it coming on, and it hurt awful too—I never imagined pain like that. We'd had a lot of good years and an enviable goodbye—Doug Napier was cheated out these both and was physically and symbolically ripped apart under the radar of justice because we thought it would be easier to make him a scapegoat than to have our community face the scrutiny and publicity of what really happened. We almost got away without anyone knowing the truth and I'm grateful to get to be the one to tell it. I don't think my telling it vindicates me of my role in that grievous wrong, but maybe the truth really does set people free. Maybe coming forward now will atone for some of the lies and tremendous wrongs we committed—if only enough that I might have a chance to be with my wife in Heaven. And that the spirit of Doug Napier might rest, if it hasn't, that he might be there too.

The final thing I need to make up for is what our silence cost the other victims and witnesses of this elusive creature known by most people as Bigfoot—the photos, files and physical proof we incinerated, witnesses we lied to and confused, what Jeffrey Green found and destroyed by that river, the misleading stories and false evidence we submitted—all of which would have exonerated Doug Napier, but also might have put to rest this centuries old argument about the existence of sasquatch.

Every so often, as I write, I find myself looking at an old sandwich bag with a finger-sized swatch of reddish-brown hair pressed flat in the airless pocket. It rests on an old file that, since that August, hasn't been opened until I decided to purge myself of this. Not even Rose-Marie knew that what was destroyed were my copies. I thought it was safer for her, not knowing.

Without the rest of the evidence, with all the skepticism and scrutiny, non-believers and nay-sayers, I'm wondering what good this last piece of the truth is?

It is proof of that thing that turned my life upside down, the morning of August 3rd, 1983.

It is proof of what we did to Napier.

After I say the last I have to say, I think the best thing is to be rid of it. I've held onto it so long, why? Because I felt guilty about Doug and wanted to hold onto something that might free him? Because I wanted proof and to be the one in control of it? Maybe because it was a constant reminder of what we did, so I could never be fully free of the guilt? After so long, I can't tell you why, but the last "maybe" is the reason why it has to go.

I don't know if anyone will believe me and maybe that hair won't give people a choice.

I think I need the skepticism now, so maybe not everyone who reads this will believe me and therefore might be undecided whether or not I am a real monster too.

PHOTO MAILED TO PATTERSON BY A BIGFOOT WITNESS
(near center of photo)

A CANVAS TENT SIMILAR TO THAT USED BY THE NAPIER FAMILY

NEAR THE RIDGE WHERE GREEN FELL

LOT NINE MARKER
(photo by author)

DESTROYED MOUNDS FOUND IN THIS AREA
A CLEAR INDICATION OF BEING IN THE VICINITY OF THE WASHOUT
(photo by author)

CHARLIE "CHUCK" HOFFMAN PAUL KETCHUM
DAVID SCHALLER (center)

JOHN KRANTZ JEFFREY GREEN

ONLY SURVIVING FRAME FROM NAPIER FAMILY CAMERA
A PHOTO OF JUNE JUST TWO DAYS BEFORE THE ATTACK

STEPHEN PATTERSON

DRAWING OF THE FOOTPRINT
FOUND AT LOT 9
(drawing by Paul Ketchum)

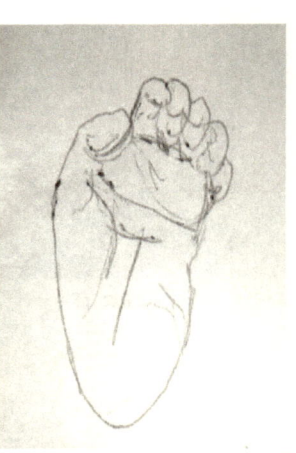

FOOTPRINT FOUND AT THE LOT 9 CRIME SCENE
(photo by author)

COPYRIGHT

NOTE FROM THE AUTHOR

The account you've just read is based upon a presumed bear attack in the Pacific Northwest and the wrongful conviction of a man, who I will not mention specifically—although this is all too common and could, essentially, be attributed to any number of cases. Because neither of those is the real reason for writing this novel, I was encouraged to publish it as fiction.

The important issue was opening people's minds to a reality that some refuse exists: one where law enforcement is not perfect (which is an unfair standard to hold them to anyway) and also a reality where we are alone in the universe, with no greater mysteries of space, spirit, or nature to discover.

ABOUT STEPHEN PATTERSON

Stephen Patterson, born and raised in Washington State, has twice retired as a reporter from one large and one small newspaper and worked within the news industry since 1929. As such, he has had the unique experience of having written articles about every war and conflict in American history since WWII as they happened.

A father of one, grandfather and great-grandfather many times over, Patterson intends to spend the rest of his days applying himself, to the best of his abilities, to those three roles—while he still has the energy.

Patterson enjoys reading, watching television, photography, loving up the grandkids, and now— hopefully—enjoying the peace and peace of mind writing this novel may bring him.